Platirius: Kikhani vs Platirius Book III

D.L. Hannah

Contents

For my Isis.

It's the third time and you're still my charm!

Chapter 1

Aiki, Queen of Kikhani, carried a tray of rancid beef and wine made with bitter herbs. One would never call her jolly, but today, she half-walked and half-skipped to where her newest guest was housed.

Were she a Human, she might have been diagnosed with histrionic personality disorder. She had a flair for the dramatic combined with a selfish streak that was positively suffocating at times.

She entered and smiled at her captive. Their eyes met and she set the tray on an old table that had seen better days with a hard *thump*. The two locked eyes for a long time, neither willing to look away first.

In the end, she became distracted, but not out of fear of the WomanForm standing before her. Her attention span was low. Selecting a chair, she carried it around the table and sat directly before her captive.

"Do you know why no one's coming for you?" she asked. She knew she wouldn't receive a response, nor did she bother waiting for one. "Nobody likes you. Your father doesn't like you. Your sister doesn't like you either."

1

She kicked the WomanForm's leg. "Your brother-in-law doesn't like you. None of your nieces like you. And your former army hopes you're dead. No one is coming to Kikhani for you...for no one wants you to return to Platirius."

General Revari smiled like a little Human girl who'd just won a national spelling bee. "I killed my father," she confessed softly. "And I killed my brother-in-law."

She kicked up dust at Queen Aiki, mimicking her mocking movements. "And I took care of my nieces, too!"

At *too*, a cloud of dust went flying into Queen Aiki's face. She didn't bother to wipe it away.

Smiling stiffly, Queen Aiki fixed General Revari with a penetrating gaze. "And I'm who they call crazy? So that's why The One knocked you off your high pedestal, eh? You're a nasty little murderer! Now, you're no longer the half-Queen of Platirius, and you're here with the Kikhanians. That's quite a fall from grace."

General Revari's eyes took in the heavy, horrific, hot pink makeup spattered on Queen Aiki's lips and face. Her shiny black outfit ended just above hot pink boots that traveled up to thighs encased in silver fishnet stockings.

A part ran from her forehead to the base of her skull. Two huge balls of hair were held together with hot pink ribbons on either side of her head. She looked like a Human prostitute from the eighties.

Queen Aiki, however, stared back as if entranced by the former Queen of Rubarius. Being held captive for hours hadn't diminished her appearance. The silk suit, accentuating the curves of her body, didn't have a single wrinkle. She wore expensive red stilettos on her small feet, and her expertly styled hair and makeup were at the peak of perfection.

"I don't think I'll kill you just yet. Why are you dressed like a Human?"

Silence.

"For a Platirian, you're a whole bundle of surprises!"

Queen Aiki laughed as if she'd just told the funniest joke in the galaxy. General Revari glared at her.

She stopped laughing and jumped out of the chair. "You think you're better than the Kikhanians, don't you? How? Your own father didn't want you!"

General Revari pursed her lips. "Where's your father?" Smirking, she waited for her to reply.

Queen Aiki's face contorted with rage. Many years ago, King Hitam left Kikhani for a Human woman he'd fallen in love with.

Queen Aiki's mother, Queen Amori, fell into a deep depression and slashed her throat open with a blade. An eight-year-old Princess Aiki watched her bleed to death on the golden floor of their palace.

Only a few weeks prior, the young princess witnessed her mother holding onto her father's legs to prevent him from leaving. King Hitam brushed his wife aside as if she were nothing more than a fly. He stared at his daughter for a long time before boarding his craft, leaving his family and Kikhani behind forever.

General Revari silently assessed her. "I don't think you have room to talk about what happens between fathers and unwanted daughters. Mine hated me, but at least he wanted me to live on Platirius. Your father left because," her voice lowered to a whisper, "he could no longer stand the sight of you and your weak-minded mother."

Lifting an impertinent brow, she said, "You allowed him to walk out on you. It would've been best if you used that blade to cut his neck open. It might've saved your mother's honor."

Queen Aiki looked at her sharply. She stood still for a moment, reflecting on her words. Finally, she cocked her head. "Don't go anywhere. I'll return shortly."

In less than ten minutes, she returned with two trays loaded with half of a roast chicken, herbed dressing, sweet potatoes swimming in honey and butter, and thick slices of apple pie a la mode.

She used her powers to release General Revari from the invisible bands around her arms and ankles. Brimming with excitement, she looked at the spread laid before them. "Come! Eat with me."

General Revari rubbed her sore arms, looking over the food warily.

"I didn't poison it!" Queen Aiki took a bite of food from both trays. "See? Come, come, sit down! I don't like cold food."

Sore from hanging in a single position for hours, General Revari gently eased her body down to sit at the table. Like a small ChildForm, Queen Aiki clapped her hands in delight.

"Isn't this nice? The lights. The ambience. Dinner is best served in my home, but I don't trust you, General Revari. If you killed your own family, who knows what you'd do to me."

General Revari's mouth curled slightly. "Touche," she said.

They ate silently for a moment before General Revari caught Queen Aiki staring pensively at her.

"Yes?"

"I'm usually not accommodating to guests, but you've been given an excellent meal. Now I want you to do something for me."

General Revari looked around at the tacky gold decorations before settling her eyes on her again. Queen Aiki was living proof that being born into royalty didn't account for good taste.

"I'm not surprised. If I were of no use to you, I would've died sooner than later."

The Queen of Kikhani simply smiled. General Revari sat back in the chair, pressing her fingers together as she imagined a dozen ways to kill her.

The nerve of Queen Aiki interrupting her plans just as she was headed to find her son. Her timing was as lousy as her taste in decorating. If she'd wanted a confrontation, she'd had years to face her. She tried to scan her mind, but it was no use. Her mind was too discombobulated to discern why she'd been brought to Kikhani.

"What do you want from me?" she asked finally.

Queen Aiki's gold eyes roamed over her. "Tell me how to kill my father."

5

P rince Justin felt as if they'd been riding in the craft for weeks. An avid science fiction and comic book fan, he assumed things moved faster in space. Apparently, they didn't.

He turned to Major Legend, who was staring out the window at a particularly beautiful purple planet. "Is that Kikhani?"

She looked over at him. Although he had more of his Human father's looks, she could easily see his mother in him. "No, that's another territory—JanIus. Kikhani is much farther."

Wiggling his eyebrows, he said, "I thought we'd be there faster than the speed of light."

She smiled wryly at his poor attempt to make a joke. In the past, she enjoyed bantering with him, but she was too worried about General Revari to humor him.

"It's painful to think how little Humans know what lies beyond Earth."

"Ouch. We might be ignorant of some things, but we have a lot of good qualities."

She patted him on the shoulder. She supposed there was some truth to that. General Revari had fallen so deeply in love with his father, she'd resigned her place as a Princess of Platirius. Of course, King Dubian's madness inspired her to embrace living with Humans.

She didn't believe there would ever be a reason to follow in her footsteps. While she disapproved of Queen Vivant being in charge of Platirius, she didn't think she'd be happy living elsewhere.

On the contrary, the reality of a permanent relocation may have been inevitable if her life lay solely in the queen's hands. She wasn't ready to die, nor would she allow the newly appointed leader of Platirius to dictate if and when her life ended.

General Lyric sat at the controls with Queen Vivant, watching Prince Justin and Major Legend quietly talking together.

"They seem rather close, don't they?"

"Hmm. Yes, I've noticed," said Queen Vivant. "I've tried to discern how much she knows about him, but she's very skilled at hiding her thoughts from me."

She directed a pointed glance toward Angela and Sheila. "She's not the only Revaltian whose mind I can't penetrate. I find it very strange. I suspect there's more going on than we realize."

General Lyric adjusted the controls of the WarCraft. "I heard King Dubian sent General Revari's InfantForm into the sun. How is it he survived?"

Queen Vivant checked the clock. They'd reach Kikhani soon. "I have no answer for that. At first, I thought she'd conspired with someone to take him and escape from Platirius. But I remember how long she grieved for him."

She was silent for a moment. "It's not possible she knew he was alive. I know her. Nothing would have stopped her from being in his life."

Gazing sorrowfully at her nephew, she sighed. "Now he's here with us and I have no idea what will happen next. He's grown to maturity on Earth. I can't imagine he'd be happy living among us. Their way of life differs so vastly from ours."

General Lyric remembered how crudely he'd spoken to her on Platirius. "Some things are different. And others certainly remain the same."

Queen Aiki was the epitome of an oddball, but her request was the last thing General Revari had expected to hear.

"Why do you want to kill your father? You've succeeded in ruling Kikhani in his place for many years. What purpose would it serve now?"

Queen Aiki mixed a bit of dressing into her sweet potatoes and took a bite.

Chewing loudly, she asked, "Why did you murder King Dubian?"

Greedily, she licked her fingers. General Revari frowned at her lack of table manners.

"I wanted to rule Platirius. But things didn't go as I expected. When Platirius split in half, I was forced to share power with Queen Vivant. That wasn't a part of the plan."

Queen Aiki swirled her fork into the dressing. "I have no siblings. I don't know how it feels to share anything with anyone." She paused, searching for a way to pose the next question. "Did you kill your mother too?"

General Revari calmly folded her hands in her lap. There were many ways to describe the strange WomanForm, but tactful wasn't one of them.

"According to King Dubian, I did. She died giving birth to me."

"Ohhh. He blamed you. Tsk. Blaming an InfantForm for her MotherForm's death. So dishonorable, but it's fitting for who he was."

She didn't want to talk about King Dubian.

"You haven't answered my question. What benefit would you reap if King Hitam is dead?"

"He's happy," she said, as if the reason was apparent. "He's been living a carefree life all this time. He hides his true identity from the silly Human women he pretends to fall in love with. Once he outlives them, he starts over in a new place with a new identity. He's been careful not to sire any ChildForms."

She didn't need to explain the reason to her—she already knew. The ChildForms he fathered would be subjected to blood testing. Any suspicious abnormalities would be reported to federal enforcement agencies that studied extraterrestrial lifeforms. He'd be tracked down, locked away, and studied like a lab animal.

However, if WomenForms procreated with Human males, the male's DNA would dominate hers. They could've raised their son without worrying had she remained on Earth with Oliver. That wasn't the case for MaleForms. The DNA of a Human woman wouldn't mask theirs—making them more susceptible to exposure.

King Hitam chose to live with Humans, but not as a science experiment. Outliving a Human lover was quite common. While Beings outside of Earth lived for millions of years, it was rare for a Human lifespan to reach over 122 years.

General Revari hadn't had time to contemplate the ramifications of outliving her husband. The decision had been taken out of her hands.

She forced herself not to concentrate on Oliver. Memories of him sent her into a dark place. There was no time for distractions. She had to get off Kikhani and get back to Platirius so she could deal with Queen Vivant.

"So what happens after you kill him? He dies, and you go back to...what? You're already the Queen of Kikhani. It doesn't make sense to end his life."

Queen Aiki started eating her pie. "Revenge is always a good motive. I don't wish to wake up another day knowing he's content while my poor mother is dead. It's disrespectful to me and to her memory."

General Revari pointed her spoon at her. "That's sweeter than the honey in these potatoes, Queen Aiki. I'm not buying it. What's the real reason for wanting him dead?"

Queen Aiki swore. *How did she know?* "It's not enough for you to be the prettier sister, is it? You want to be the smarter one too."

The signature red light in General Revari's eyes took on a sinister gleam. "I am *everything* Queen Vivant isn't. But what would you know about intellect? You've missed the mark your entire life."

"Ah, what a brash and vain WomanForm you are. Tsk. A MaleForm would have difficulty living with you and your overinflated ego."

"Insulting me isn't going to motivate me to help you. If I were you, I'd stop now."

Queen Aiki figured she'd better not push her luck. "Well, after all this time living on Earth, he's decided to be a FatherForm again. He's found a way to procreate without detection."

General Revari crossed her arms over her breasts. "Oh? Go on."

"His current position permits him to manipulate the results of any tests performed on his heirs. He destroyed my family. He shouldn't be allowed to make another."

She reflected on Queen Aiki's words. "Has he impregnated anyone yet?"

"Not yet. But he's met a silly young Human woman and is desperate to get her pregnant."

"Why now?"

Queen Aiki gnawed on a chicken bone. "He's dying. Living among Humans for thousands of years has led to severe immunocompromising. His self-regenerating powers have been corrupted. So he's no longer immune to their diseases."

Gallium had told General Revari about an ancient battle between Platirius and Kikhani. After King Hitam impaled a young Major Kron's neck with a blade, a vicious kick from Major Kron sent him flying.

With blood gushing from a near-fatal wound, he led Platirius into victory against Kikhani and was appointed to general. Years later, General Revari fought many battles under his command.

She'd never witnessed any MaleForm fight as skillfully as the former General of Platirius.

He'd still be alive had he not betrayed me.

Hiding a smile, she turned her attention back to Queen Aiki.

"Calculating by Earth's time, he has less than five hundred days to live. He aims to create a new life and drain its powers to heal himself. He'll make it seem as if the half-Human infant never had a chance to survive. It's how he plans to sustain his life."

She tried to gauge what General Revari was thinking. She hoped that once she revealed King Hitam's plan to sacrifice an innocent life, she'd help her stop him.

General Revari put down her fork. After thinking for a moment, she asked, "What's in it for me?"

"Your freedom."

She laughed in her face. "Are you serious? You think I can't leave Kikhani without helping you kill King Hitam?"

"You are a skilled warrior, General Revari. Your reputation in battle precedes you. However, you're in my domain now. What I say is law here. If I order your head sliced into four even pieces and served to me on a platter, it will be done."

"But you won't. We both know I'm the only one who can pull off killing a Being as powerful as King Hitam. You amuse yourself by reminding me I'm not well-liked, but neither are you. No MaleForm in the galaxy will marry you because you're eccentric. Sporadic. Unpredictable. Your moods fluctuate worse than the weather."

She pushed her empty plates away. "Although they'd never admit it, most MaleForms fear you. They don't know if you'll passionately kiss your husband in the morning only to slit his treasure off by nightfall. That's your specialty—gelding MaleForms who displease you."

She made a face. "You even hang their treasures over your mantel. You've built quite a reputation for yourself—for being mentally unstable."

Queen Aiki cupped her chin in her hand. "What an interesting assessment coming from someone who was locked away in Platirius's Chamber of Despair."

"That doesn't mean I belonged there. You're free only because you haven't been caught. Who on Kikhani is bold enough to challenge you for the throne?"

She grinned at General Revari. "You're right. No one is. Yet...since your plan to rule Platirius failed...I wonder if you'd be dubious enough to challenge Queen Vivant for the throne?"

"It doesn't matter to me what The One has proclaimed. I'd rather see her dead than rule Platirius."

"It has been prophesied that if Queen Vivant dies, the new ruler will come from Kikhani."

"Correct. Since you've kidnapped me, that places me in the perfect position to win back Platirius."

Queen Aiki's smile vanished. "I've ruled Kikhani for hundreds of years. Why shouldn't I have the right to kill Queen Vivant and lead Platirius?"

General Revari's eyes narrowed. "I have plans for my sister. If you get in my way, I'll take your head before I take hers. I'll help you kill King Hitam...on one condition."

Queen Aiki sat back in her chair, sated from the excellently prepared meal. "Yes?" she purred. "What may the Queen of Kikhani do for you?"

"*If* I help you kill him, you must agree to assist me in getting rid of her. Then, we'll both have what we want. You, a dead father, and to remain on the throne of Kikhani. As the ruler of Platirius, I'd spit on the corpse of my sister in front of General Lyric. And this time, I won't be interfering in The One's affairs. That means He won't interfere in mine."

She watched as Queen Aiki collected the supper dishes.

"We could continue being mortal enemies or form a permanent alliance to benefit both planets. If we combined our forces, we'd wage war against all the galactic kings and conquer their territories. Then, the entire galaxy would be controlled by WomenForms. Platirius would control the east, and Kikhani would take the west."

Queen Aiki's golden eyes beamed with excitement. "General Revari, I love the way you think!"

Prince Justin gazed out the window at the breathtaking expanse of space. Although Major Legend had kept him abreast of his identity, he wondered if reuniting with his birth mother would be a positive experience.

Not wanting to hurt his adoptive parents, he'd kept pictures of his biological parents hidden. Only in the stillness of the night would he take them out, staring at them for hours. At times, he'd wished they were a real family.

According to Major Legend, his mother had been forbidden to raise him as punishment for falling in love with his father. Dr. Justin Ascencio, now Prince Justin of the formidable royal family of Platirius, had never been in love.

To an outside observer, that would've been hard to believe. He'd inherited his height, dimples, and green eyes from his father, but he had his mother's smile. He was a good-looking man with a successful career as a brain surgeon.

Women of all ages coveted being the one who'd win his heart. Repeatedly, they all failed. He didn't need to reflect on why—he already knew.

His mother's absence had left him deeply scarred. Fearing rejection and abandonment, he purposely hadn't allowed any of the women he dated to get close to him. He dove into his career—sometimes working up to eighty hours a week. Unable to heal his broken heart, he pushed himself to be the best in his field.

A natural prodigy, he breezed through accelerated classes and entered medical school at a young age. The coursework had come easily to him. However, enduring the scorn and envy of his older male peers had been challenging.

He lost count of the times he'd been accused of cheating on his exams. They couldn't accept that a younger, more attractive man born outside of their country quickly excelled in areas they struggled with.

Dr. Cornelius Johnson had been a staunch supporter of his. Once he caught wind of the bullying, he shielded him from their unwarranted attacks and ensured his ascension to the top wasn't undermined. As the chief physician, no one wanted to mince words with him.

He had the power to make or break a career in medicine and wielded his influence on more than one occasion to demonstrate how lethal he could be if one crossed him. Eventually, jealousy succumbed to fear, and Justin was left alone.

He wondered what Dr. Johnson would think of his birth mother. More importantly, how would *he* feel once they were face to face? His gaze drifted over to General Lyric. He thought she was lovely. She was precisely the type of woman he felt comfortable with.

She had charmed him with her beauty and an aloofness that kept him at a distance. She didn't hang on his every word or pretend to be shy and unassuming. He eschewed those types of women.

He didn't like playing games, nor did he allow women to play with his head. If he were honest, what happened to his parents terrified him. He couldn't imagine being ripped apart from his loved ones.

The forces of the old kings showed him that Queen Vivant had lost three daughters. He struggled with what he'd said to her. The cruelty behind his words surprised him. Embracing apathy—believing she deserved to suffer for her role in ruining his family—was new and unsettling to him.

He took an oath to practice non-maleficence. He firmly believed every life was precious. Yet, after inheriting the powers of his ancestors, he felt an unrelenting coldness brewing within him.

Madness threatened to reach out from the darkness, consuming all that he was. He suspected the answer was in his right hand—King Dubian's BrainStaff.

As for King Dubian, his voice was among those that swam deep within his psyche. Queen Vivant had been his treasured child, while his mother had borne the brunt of his scorn. He tried to ignore the voices.

There would be no favoritism extended toward his aunt. In fact, he intended to use the dead kings' powers to right past wrongs. Once his mother was back on top where she belonged, he hoped it would make King Dubian roast more evenly in hell.

"Kikhani is coming up on our radar," said General Lyric. "We're almost there."

Queen Vivant stood up, taking in the golden planet. "Grab your weapons and get ready. This will be no surprise attack. The Kikhanians purposely left their protective shield open. They knew we'd come for General Revari." Her BrainStaff glowed a vibrant blue, highlighting the fierceness in her silver eyes.

"Remember to work as a single unit," she warned. "If the enemy detects the slightest weakness in us, then we'll all die. Have I been heard?"

Thunderous cheers echoed throughout the WarCraft. The Vivacians and Revaltians were ready.

An eerie emptiness met their arrival. General Lyric scanned the perimeter but didn't see a single Kikhanian warrior. Heightening her senses, she moved steadily ahead of the rest of the soldiers.

"Be wary of your surroundings," she said. "They're waiting for us."

Chapter 2

A voice rang out from high hills covered in fine golden dust. "I hate it when someone shows up at my home unannounced."

It was Queen Aiki.

"Don't you know it's rude not to call first?"

She glared at the intruders. "Kikhanians!" she commanded. "Show them how hospitable we are!"

A gold ray fired through the chest of a Vivacian soldier. She fell face-first at General Lyric's feet.

"Platirians!" shouted General Lyric. "Take cover!"

"Bring me the head of Queen Vivant!" ordered Queen Aiki. "Or her arm. Or leg. It doesn't matter. And make her scream. I want to hear it in my dreams when I sleep tonight."

"If you want my head so badly, why not come and get it yourself?" asked Queen Vivant, holding up her BrainStaff.

"I would...But I don't have any lubricant to protect my face."

"With a face that hideous, it's the lubricant that needs protection."

Queen Aiki's head snapped up like a lizard. "You arrogant whore! Millions of MaleForms desire me!"

Queen Vivant nodded. "Yes. I've heard your face is a popular prop for target practice."

Queen Aiki fumed at the laughing Platirians soldiers. She hated being the butt of someone's joke. She moved her head from behind a hill just enough for Queen Vivant to see the fire burning in her eyes.

"I'm gonna dissect you like a frog and eat your legs," she promised.

Queen Vivant smirked. "Try me, dear. I'll make it worth your while."

With the speed of a golden eagle, Queen Aiki ducked from her BrainStaff's blast. Dozens of Kikhanian soldiers stormed down the hills, crashing into the waiting Platirians. The sweet sound of battle coursed through Kikhani as the WomenForms fought valiantly.

Suddenly, a wave of vertigo flowed over the soldiers, lifting the Kikhanians high above the heads of their enemies. They hovered in the air seconds before crashing into the ground. Repeatedly, they were lifted and hurled onto the battlefield, their cries vibrating in the darkness.

"What is that?!" shouted Queen Aiki, pointing at a figure levitating in the air.

Some of the Kikhanians tried to struggle to their feet on crushed and broken limbs to see what their queen referred to. Shikay, a Kikhanian soldier, looked up into space. *A MaleForm*! Unseen hands wrapped around her throat, twisting her neck until it broke with a sharp *snap*.

Queen Aiki's furious gaze shifted back to Queen Vivant. "You brought a MaleForm to my domain?! You and your sister declared no WomenForms would fight along with MaleForms, yet you have one in your army! You spineless traitor!"

Amused, Queen Vivant smiled at her. "He doesn't belong to Platirius. I'm borrowing him to crush you and your army. And, Queen Aiki? The day I owe you any explanation will be when I close my eyes for good."

"Oh, that day has come! You will not leave here alive!"

Unmoved, Queen Vivant stared up at the crazed WomanForm. "You're still yapping, space hound? Get to biting!" She looked up at Prince Justin hovering over them. "Cover me. I'm going for Queen Aiki's head!"

"Bring me that MaleForm's treasure!" commanded Queen Aiki. "Keep it in one piece!"

He nodded to Queen Vivant as all Kikhanian eyes fell on him. He swerved effortlessly, returning fire as the WomenForm warriors rushed to take him down. Queen Vivant reached the top of the hill, colliding with Queen Aiki at full speed.

"You...pampered horse!" screeched Queen Aiki. The two Queens clashed BrainStaffs and swords as the battle waged on.

A Kikhanian jumped on Prince Justin's back. "You're going to wish you'd never come here, MaleForm!"

He grabbed her by the collar and slammed her to the ground. After scanning her face, he grimaced. Unlike Platirius, ugly didn't begin to describe the females of Kikhani.

21

"The only thing I regret is not getting a prettier opponent. I've never believed in hitting women, but since you look like a man, it makes it a bit easier."

Queen Vivant knocked Queen Aiki's BrainStaff out of her hands and pinned her to the ground. "Where's my sister?"

Queen Aiki grinned up at her. "She's where she belongs. Locked away in our confinement chamber."

Queen Vivant placed her sword to her neck. "You're going to take me to her. Now!"

"No, I don't think I will, Queen Vivant."

"Then I'll cut your head off and hold it up for all your army to see. You know what that means, don't you?"

"It means," said a voice coming from behind her, "you'll absorb Kikhani into Platirius. We can't have that now, can we?"

Queen Vivant felt a sharp bolt of pain go up her spine. She rolled over Queen Aiki, who got up and kicked her down to the bottom of the hill. She looked up to see who had ambushed her.

"General Revari! You're working with Queen Aiki?"

"Did you finally figure it out, big sister? You should know by now I'm willing to take any chance to bring you down," she said, raising her BrainStaff to her face. "Now you die."

"Queen Vivant!" cried General Lyric.

General Revari turned and shot expertly at a soldier, but was grabbed by the throat and slammed into the hard curvature of high ground. A hard blow to her face enraged her. She raised her BrainStaff again, but Queen Vivant said, "No, General Revari! He's your son!"

Stunned, she lowered the BrainStaff seconds before another strike sent her spiraling into darkness. Prince Justin had heard what Queen Vivant said, but it was too late. He'd already struck her. Swiftly, he rushed to General Revari, who lay sprawled on the ground.

"Why didn't you tell me who she was sooner?" he shouted at Queen Vivant. "I could've killed her!"

"Roll her off to the side," she commanded. "We still have the Kikhanians to contend with!"

He looked over his shoulder. Queen Aiki's soldiers were coming full force for him. Being a MaleForm and possessing advanced powers made him more of a threat. Quickly, he gathered General Revari and flew with her into a cave deep within a mountain.

As the Kikhanians tried to blast their way in, he ascended from the top of the cave, firing on them. Panicked, Queen Aiki watched him kill a group of her soldiers with a single blast.

Queen Revari had a MaleForm child? And he's more powerful than all of us!

Queen Aiki ran to General Revari and slapped her hard in the face. "Wake up! Wake up! That brat of yours is killing my soldiers. You must stop him!"

She groaned. She felt as if she'd been hit by a WarCraft at full speed.

Queen Vivant's voice came rushing back to her.

He's your son!

Immediately, she jumped to her feet and ran out of the cave just as Queen Vivant was getting to her feet.

"What did you say his name was?" she asked.

"Prince Justin," panted Queen Vivant. "He has father's BrainStaff!"

"What? How did that happen? It was supposed to be shipped off into the sun with King Dubian!"

"I kept it," said Queen Vivant quietly.

General Revari stared at her. "You idiot! You would want a keepsake of his. You know how powerful it is! It should've been burned with him!"

"Well, it wasn't. Now it's in the hands of your son, and it's made him more powerful than anyone could ever imagine. I hate agreeing with Queen Aiki, but she's right. You have to stop him."

They looked up at him flying over the Kikhanians. "The more WomenForms he kills, the more his power increases. We may not be able to defend ourselves if the battle continues."

General Revari scowled. "Imbecile."

As she watched him hovering above them, a myriad of emotions rushed through her. He had his father's looks and her acumen for battle. It looked as if he'd fought countless wars instead of debuting as a soldier.

"Prince Justin, stand down!" she ordered.

Briefly, he trained his attention on her. "Stand down? Do you see all these women trying to kill me?"

General Revari turned to Queen Aiki. "Order your troops to stop firing on my son. Or our deal is off."

The fury on Queen Aiki's face was plain. "Kikhanians! Stop firing on the MaleForm!"

The sea of fire ceased as the Kikhanian and Platirian armies pulled back. Standing toe to toe, neither dared to take their eyes off their opponent.

"We wouldn't have come if I had known you two were so friendly. It appears you don't need rescuing, sister."

"I've never needed you. But you didn't waste a trip. You can take my place as Queen Aiki's prisoner, and I'll leave with my son."

Queen Vivant chuckled. It amazed her how her sister's arrogance rivaled their father's.

"That isn't going to happen. I've allowed him to use father's BrainStaff, but as the *true* ruler of Platirius,"—she raised her arm, sending King Dubian's BrainStaff flying to her outstretched hand—"this belongs to me."

Without the power of the BrainStaff, he could no longer fly. Helpless, he plummeted out of the sky. General Revari ran and caught him before he hit the ground.

"Oh man," he said. "I feel wiped out."

He passed out in her arms.

Trying not to panic, she looked from him to Queen Vivant. "What have you done to him?"

Queen Vivant shrugged one shoulder. "Nothing. As long as he holds King Dubian's BrainStaff, he may wield its power. But not without my permission. Now that the power has worn off, he's back to normal. So, you had plans to keep me here?" She shook her head in disgust. "Let me assure you, if you try to capture me, I will not hesitate to take him back to Platirius and lock him up in our confinement chamber.

The Vivacians moved closer to him. "And I could easily do it," said Queen Vivant. "The Kikhanians won't try and stop me. He's a MaleForm—a threat to their way of life. He'll never be welcome here."

General Revari lowered him to the ground, wiping sweat from his brow. Still wary, the soldiers looked down at him. One word from either of their commanders would've resulted in a swift death.

She looked around at them. "The first one who touches my son will be the first head I take," she promised.

The Kikhanian soldiers looked to her, their eyes blazing with fury. Queen Vivant was right. They despised the MaleForm, but she was hated more for birthing him. No one would fight to protect him.

"It appears we're no longer needed here, General Lyric," said Queen Vivant. "Gather all the soldiers, including everyone who copulated with Simonius on the WarCraft. We're going home."

"We aren't going back with you, Queen Vivant," said Major Legend defiantly. "You can't force us to return to Platirius with you!"

"Who is going to stop me?" asked Queen Vivant coolly.

Major Legend turned pleadingly to General Revari. "You can't allow her to take us back to Platirius! She'll kill us!" She circled her arm to include the half-dozen soldiers who shared her fate. "We've remained loyal to you, General Revari! Please let us stay with you."

"Why are you asking her if you may stay on my planet?" asked Queen Aiki. "General Revari isn't in charge of Kikhani. I am."

General Revari looked out at the soldiers. "Platirius may be one planet again, but I'm still the leader of the Revaltians. Half the warriors you brought here today are still under my command. There's more than enough left of Queen Aiki's army. You're vastly outnumbered if I add the number of my Revaltians who are still on Earth."

Her red gaze glowed with hostility. "If you've forgotten what the Surveyors said, I'll remind you. My Revaltians will follow me until death, not you. You may be the Queen of Platirius, but on Kikhani, you're nothing. Please give me a reason for having General Lyric killed before your eyes."

Queen Vivant shook her head. "You should concentrate on forming a bond with your son and leave Platirian business to me."

General Revari slightly positioned her body so his head rested on her thighs. "No, you should leave *my* son to *me*. No one should be forced to serve under you if they do not wish to do so. Was it not you who said you'd never rule Platirius by fear and force as King Dubian had? The Revaltians are staying with me."

Queen Vivant's grip on her BrainStaff tightened. "No, General Revari. They broke the most sacred of Platirian laws. It will not go unpunished."

General Revari pointed to Major Legend. "Legend saved my son while you stood by and watched King Dubian try to kill him. Surely you're not dancing on your high pedestal of justice now?"

Queen Vivant knew what General Revari was trying to do, but it wouldn't work. She wouldn't let her guilt prevent her from performing her duty.

"I'm not letting them stay."

Queen Aiki stepped between the sisters. "What's this? Are you two so spoiled you think you command the whole galaxy? The decision isn't up to you."

She glared at Queen Vivant before turning to General Revari. "Or you if they remain on Kikhani."

General Revari turned to her. "You'll need more protection for Kikhani if we're going to Earth to accomplish your little mission."

Queen Vivant raised a curious brow. "What mission?"

General Revari gave her a frosty glance. "None of your business."

"I would've thought you learned your lesson by now. As Earth's protector, anything involving it is my business."

"Not this time," said Queen Aiki. "Kikhani's issues are my concern, not yours. You will not interfere, Queen Vivant. Or I'll kill your general right now. If you're wise, you'll take the soldiers who are foolish enough to serve you and leave my planet. Any who served under General Revari may remain."

"And what will you do about him?" asked Queen Vivant, pointing to Prince Justin. "Even without our father's BrainStaff, he still has the power to overthrow you. He gains strength by copulating with WomenForms."

She turned and pointed to the Revaltians. "Many here are guilty of that already. If he succeeds, then your reign is over. He'll learn all your secrets and turn them against you. Is that something you want to take a gamble on?"

General Revari pointed at her. "You leave my son out of this! He's my responsibility, not yours. You had a chance to be a MotherForm. You failed. Remember?"

Major Legend looked uncomfortably away as Queen Vivant stilled. "I'm going to try and forget you said that. Never mention my daughters again."

General Revari gave her a cold smile. "Gladly...Your Highness."

She addressed her with such venom that Queen Vivant almost fired on her, but she controlled herself. She knew how to push her buttons. After losing her daughters, she found it less easy to control her temper than she had in the past.

Clearly aware she was being baited, she refused to allow General Revari to make her lose control. General Lyric noticed Major Legend nervously shifting from one foot to another.

She knows something about the princesses.

Queen Vivant hated to admit she'd been defeated. She planned to bring enough soldiers to infiltrate Kikhani and return with General Revari. Now, the general had turned the tables on her. She wanted to force them to return to Platirius, but she was outnumbered. It wasn't worth losing more innocent lives.

Although she didn't intend to allow Major Legend and the others to get away with what they'd done, they were on enemy territory. Now wasn't the time to exert her authority. They had to retreat. It seemed Queen Aiki had further plans with General Revari.

"We'll call a draw this time, Queen Aiki. Neither you nor I claimed victory today. We shall leave Kikhani now."

Queen Aiki gave her an evil smile. "A sagacious decision, Queen Vivant. I'd gladly hang your head above my mantel if I didn't already have more important affairs. But for now, I'll agree to a stalemate. Just know, once my assignment is completed, I'll finish you off for good."

Queen Vivant looked coolly from Queen Aiki to General Revari. "I look forward to it. Vivacians, let us leave Kikhani."

Queen Aiki, the Kikhanians, and General Revari watched as the Platirians entered the WarCraft. They watched until it was completely out of sight.

Queen Aiki turned to General Revari, who still held Prince Justin in her arms. "How do I know what Queen Vivant said isn't true? If he threatens my soldiers, he cannot remain here."

General Revari stroked his brow. "You needn't worry about my son. I won't allow any of you to hurt him."

Queen Aiki nodded. "Very well. You and I will leave for Earth soon. As for what's left of your former army, I expect them to follow Kikhanian law. If they don't, there will be trouble."

Fury blazed in General Revari's eyes. It had been a long time since she'd taken orders. She had no problem letting Queen Aiki know she wouldn't boss her around.

"And if you want them to help protect Kikhani in your absence, I expect your soldiers to treat mine with respect. They're not here to bow to you or them. How will you hold up your end of the bargain now that you've allowed Queen Vivant to leave?"

Queen Aiki ignored the challenge in General Revari's tone. She'd learned playing dumb was the key to accomplishing her goals. She was actually much more clever than she was given credit for. But...if she wanted King Hitam dead, she'd have to play the game. At least for a while.

"You will kill King Hitam as you promised. If your son returns to Earth, she cannot hold him over your head. Then, we'll gather every soldier here and attack Platirius. You're still a Platirian. We'll use your *nued* points to lower Platirius's protective shield and strike when she least expects it."

"How do you know she won't return to Kikhani once we leave for Earth?" She looked over at Major Legend and the other Revaltian soldiers who had copulated with Simonius. "My sister is no fool. They were dubious right under our noses. She's not going to let it go so easily."

Queen Aiki looked in the direction Queen Vivant's WarCraft had taken. "I have no way of knowing what she will or won't do once I leave Kikhani. But if she returns, I intend to lay out a welcome mat she won't forget."

Queen Vivant sat with the Vivacians while they cleaned their gear. Now that she was back to her old self, General Lyric struggled to confess what she'd suspected for months.

Although Queen Vivant had been under the effects of the CallePepper, she'd sensed the sporadic rhythm of General Lyric's emotions. Unfortunately, her powers had been severely muted. She blamed herself for not being able to help the WomenForms who looked up to her.

"Something has been disturbing you for a while, General Lyric," said Queen Vivant. "Now is the appropriate time to tell me what it is."

General Lyric hesitated. For months, the queen's recovery had been the most important goal. Everyone made sure not to say or do anything that might undermine her well-being. Now she was strong and healthy again, but General Lyric was afraid of causing a setback.

"I...I don't want to upset you."

Queen Vivant grimaced, rubbing her temples. She had a pounding headache.

General Lyric touched her hand. "Should I have one of the medical staff bring something to ease your headache?"

"No. I'm still recovering from the CallePepper." She smiled bitterly. "I probably will be for the rest of my lifespan. I can't afford to take any substances—not even for routine things."

She bit her lip. "And I'm already upset, General Lyric. Too much has happened. Now I must find a way to make it all right again. You might as well come out with it. What's done in the dark always comes to light."

General Lyric sighed. It had been such a heavy burden suspecting General Revari of murdering the princesses. She still had no proof she was responsible. What if she were wrong?

She took a deep breath. *It's best to just get it all out in the open.*

"I think General Revari planned the murder of your daughters." Looking into her eyes, she said, "And I think she used the Human to do it."

Queen Vivant's gaze was unwavering. "You think or you know, Lyric? That's a pretty hefty accusation."

"I know General Revari took the CallePepper to Earth and used it as a weapon against the Humans. She called it Allebri. She also used it on you. I believe she murdered the princesses so it would look as if grief were driving you mad instead of the CallePepper."

General Lyric finished cleaning her sword and placed it back in its scabbard. "She was the only one who stood to gain something from all of it. She's hated you for years."

A wave of nausea came over Queen Vivant. "No one is more aware of that than I. But to kill my daughters?" She let out a heavy sigh. "We never had the opportunity to question the Human. Platirian law forbade it. He said he couldn't remember when or why he came to Platirius. I'll admit I haven't stopped wondering about that."

General Lyric laced up a fresh pair of boots. "He was a cover. A mark to be used to take control of Earth. Then she made sure he'd be disposed of before his memory returned."

Queen Vivant exhaled softly. "Sonee scanned his brain but didn't find anything."

Sergeant Thea saluted General Lyric and Queen Vivant. "All of the uniforms and weapons have been properly sanitized, General."

"Thank you, Sergeant Thea," said General Lyric. Sergeant Thea saluted her again and bowed to Queen Vivant before making a quick exit. General Lyric stood with one hand on her hip, thinking.

"That means Cyan, Cita, or Jia was behind it. If they used magic to hide their tracks, it explains the lapses in his memory and why our surveillance couldn't track him as he moved in and out of the chambers. She had a free pass to Earth with you out of the way. There was no one to stop her."

A slight chill coursed through Queen Vivant.

Could it be true? Could my sister be responsible for the murders of my daughters?

She certainly had a motive to carry it out. General Revari believed she wanted her infant son to die. She hadn't. Yet, she'd been powerless to stop King Dubian from harming him.

General Revari knew she was responsible for King Dubian finding her, but she refused to believe her sister hadn't possessed the power to defy their father. How could she? Queen Vivant was young and had fallen deeply in love with General Kron. Marriage was her ticket to freedom—or so she'd thought.

Had Queen Vivant revolted against King Dubian's will, he would've severed her engagement to General Kron. Her dream of becoming queen would've been halted. What's worse, her precious daughters would've never been born.

King Dubian had complete control over everything and everyone in his kingdom. How could her sister not see it?

She was glad General Revari had been reunited with her son. But...if General Lyric was correct in suspecting her of being the mastermind behind the murders, the former Revaltians wouldn't be the only ones she'd confiscate and punish. General Revari would be arrested for treason and sentenced to pay for her crimes. No matter the cost.

Chapter 3

General Revari could not stop looking at her son. He was gorgeous—a perfect mesh of her and Oliver. Eyes she never thought she'd see again stared back at her. She saw many questions reflected in them. She couldn't remember ever feeling so elated.

"Are you hungry? I could have something prepared for you in the dining chamber, or I'll cook for you. You may have whatever you like."

Twin smiles met each other. He chuckled. "Spoken like a true mother," he told her.

The sheen of tears in her eyes caught his breath. He hadn't expected this iron-hard woman to be capable of vulnerability.

"No, thank you. I'm not hungry right now. Not for food anyway."

Her fingers danced on her thighs. She could hardly keep still.

"Then what is it? Just tell me and it will be done."

"Maybe you can clear something up for me?"

She placed a hand on his strong arm. It felt wonderful to touch him. *Her son was alive*!

"Anything. You have only to name it."

He gave her hand a gentle squeeze. "Am I really a prince?"

She nodded. "Yes. You're my son. That makes you royalty. It's your birthright."

He rubbed the stubble on his chin. He needed to shave. What were the chances of him finding a decent razor on Kikhani? Queen Aiki's soldiers were ugly, but at least they weren't bearded.

"Where's King Dubian?"

"More dead than the moon," she said.

He noted the gleam of satisfaction in her eye. He didn't want to ask the next question, but curiosity was getting the better of him. "How did he die?"

She wondered if she should tell him the truth. Now that the dark magic of the former kings was gone, he didn't remember anything about Platirius. She decided to be honest with him and allow him to determine whether or not he wanted to remain in her life.

"I killed him." He didn't say anything, so she continued. "After I got rid of him, Platirius split into two realms. Its power was divided between Queen Vivant and me."

With a spinning head, he lurched forward. He wasn't expecting to hear what she'd just confessed to.

"Why did you do it?"

"He ordered your father to be tortured and murdered. And...I thought he ended you too. I was enraged and fell deeply into depression. Over time, my thirst for vengeance consumed me.

So...I made plans to kill him. I refused to allow him to live after what he took from me."

She took both of his hands in hers. They were larger than hers and felt much warmer.

"I killed Queen Vivant's husband too. And...after losing her daughters, she has no one now."

Shaking his head as if coming out of a trance, he blinked. "Are you sorry for what you've done?"

"No," she said quickly. "I'd do it again if I had the opportunity."

She meant it. She'd taken great care to see that King Dubian and General Kron had paid for taking Oliver away from her. Both had earned what they received. Watching Queen Vivant mourn for them had been more than gratifying. General Revari felt vindicated in avenging her husband's death. Still, her sister had to pay the debt she owed her. In blood.

He didn't realize his grip had tightened on her, but she didn't mind.

"Why kill her husband?"

"At the time, he was the General of Platirius and the next in line to the throne. My husband—your father—was tortured and killed on his watch. He called my Oliver trash...to my face. Your father was kind and peaceful. He didn't deserve to die that way, but General Kron earned his fate."

"I guess I can understand that...but..."

The evil forces of his ancestors surging within him while he'd possessed the BrainStaff had muted his sense of integrity.

Now that they were gone, he struggled to comprehend how his mother could murder three innocent girls.

She read his mind. "Don't worry about the princesses. What's done is done."

"Mama," he said softly.

Hearing him call her *Mama* warmed her heart.

"I'll understand if you want nothing to do with me. For me, killing is as easy as breathing. I still feel my actions were justified." She held his gaze. "I'll never be sorry for what I've done."

"Does she know you murdered her family?"

Releasing his hands, she stood up and stretched. It had been a long day.

"No. She doesn't know I'm responsible."

"Then, if she finds out...what will she do to you?"

She shrugged. "She'll try to have me arrested and executed. I wouldn't worry about that. She'll die long before that happens. She's the only one left who hasn't paid for what happened to Oliver. No matter how long it takes, I'll make her suffer."

"We agree on that. I'm not on board with everything you've done, but I won't let anything happen to you. The old man and General Whatever His Name Is got what they had coming to them. But the girls didn't deserve to die, Mama."

Standing at a mirror, she wove her long hair into a knot and secured it with a pin that belonged to Queen Dellah. After King Dubian died, she had removed everything that belonged to her mother from his bed chamber.

Except for photos. Her sneaky father had hidden them in Queen Vivant's wedding trunk. Once she killed her, she'd take them too.

"I said not to worry about them. There's no going back now, son."

"My mission is to keep you safe," he said.

He sounded so serious that the irony behind their sudden reunion made her laugh.

Amused, he asked, "What's so funny?"

"My baby wants to protect me. It's my job to protect you."

He scanned her features. "For someone who's five million years old, you look amazing. I expected a little old lady to be my mom."

He didn't want to hurt her, but he wanted her to see him as a man, not the infant she lost years ago.

"Mama, I'm not a baby anymore. You saw how well I did out there fighting all those hideous women." The scarlet glow of her BrainStaff caught his attention. "By the way, how do I get a BrainStaff?"

She whirled to face him. "Major Legend told you how old I am?"

He doubled over in laughter despite her ignoring his declaration of autonomy.

"So women care about age even in outer space? That's wild!"

Her curiosity piqued, she ruffled his curly hair. "WomenForms. How much has she told you about me?"

He paused to think. "She said you loved me, but your family wanted me dead. She also said they didn't treat you right. She gave me pictures of you and Dad and said one day I'd meet you in person. Aunt Legend has been very good to me. She never missed a birthday or a graduation."

Memories of the good times he'd shared with Major Legend brought a smile to his face. "She told me she wanted to be there for me since you couldn't. I'm very grateful to her for staying in my life. Without her, I never would've known about you or where I really came from."

She still had business to address with Major Legend. King Dubian never sent WomenForms to Earth for special missions. He thought they were too incompetent. That meant she'd risked death every time she left Platirius. General Revari hadn't known how much she'd sacrificed to protect her son.

Over the years, General Revari had placed her life on the line for her soldiers many times. Shunned and despised by her own family, she had created a group of WomenForms not merely to take orders; the Revaltians were a sisterhood.

Hence, she refused to accept less than absolute respect and loyalty from her army. She was eager to speak with some of the Revaltians and address their traitorous actions.

He tried to gauge her mood, but it was difficult to tell what she was thinking. "Mama?"

She pulled herself out of her reverie, turning her focus on him. "Yes? Oh, you asked about a BrainStaff. You'd have to take a planet by killing a ruler. I won't allow it."

Shocked, he asked, "Why not? Didn't you see how well I fought out there?"

She nodded. "I did. You made me proud today, but this isn't your home. You belong on Earth. If you tried to claim a planet, they'd kill you. Then I'd have to go killing everyone again. Humans—even half ones—are despised here. No galactic king will allow a half-Human to take over his planet. There's no place for you in the galaxy. I'm sorry."

His disappointment turned into excitement when she handed him an elaborately carved platinum razor. "A souvenir from a king I killed in battle. It was one of his most prized possessions."

Grateful, he took it. Scrutinizing it, he was pleased with the workmanship. He'd never seen anything like it. "Thank you—this is awesome! Do you have more like this?"

She nodded proudly. "Yes. I've collected well over five hundred artifacts."

He frowned. "They belong to people you've killed?"

She cocked her head. "Of course. How else would I have obtained them?"

He grimaced. *Hi, my name is Justin, and my mother is a serial killer.*

She scanned his mind again. "Killing is a natural part of life, son. No one lives forever."

He decided to let what she said roll off his back. "Well, I don't know if you know, but an Apocalypse is happening on Earth, Mom. I don't know if I want to be subjected to plagues and forced to take the beast's mark."

She sat next to him, enjoying the warmth of his Human form. "After I lost the right to rule Platirius, I was on my way to find you. I didn't stick around to find out what happened on Earth. Don't worry about the Apocalypse. I can protect you from that."

She clasped her small hands together. "Kikhani once had a MaleForm ruler. He forfeited his position when he chose to live on Earth."

He sat up straight. "An Alien is running around Earth?"

"There are many so-called *Aliens* there. We've been on Earth since the beginning of time. Humans would've never advanced as far as they have without intervention from galactic Beings."

He wondered how many people he'd met who looked Human but weren't. Had they worked by his side?

God...had he slept with any Aliens?

"Although Queen Aiki epitomizes insanity, the WomenForms have become accustomed to following her. One of her flaws is having an unhealthy obsession with MaleForms."

"What do you mean?"

"She loves copulating with them. Then she kills them."

He stopped admiring the blade. "Please tell me you're not thinking what I think you are."

She rolled her eyes. "Do you think I'd let that beast harm you? Major Legend may have filled you in on some things, but you have much to learn about me."

"Then...would you marry again? Is there someone you've fallen for?"

"Bite your tongue, ChildForm. There will never be another for me besides your father."

"Hm. Gallium seems to like you."

She coughed and sputtered. "Gallium? Don't confuse loyalty for love. There will never be anything between him and I. Speaking of Gallium..."

"What?"

General Revari smiled. A genuine smile.

Exasperated, Dr. Barrios paced the floor of the confinement chamber. Amused, Gallium watched him while setting up another round of the game they'd spent hours playing.

"I can't believe you're still focused on playing a game while Queen Vivant and her mindless vermin have returned from Kikhani without General Revari!"

Gallium looked up at his eldest brother. As ChildForms, he'd always been the calmer of the two. Seeing no reason to panic, he carefully arranged the pieces on the board.

"Do you want to go first or should I?"

Dr. Barrios didn't break stride. "Gallium, my mind isn't on playing anymore. Did you hear what I said?"

Gallium shrugged. "Yes, I heard you. I don't think there's any reason to be alarmed."

Dr. Barrios stopped pacing and gaped at him. "No reason to be alarmed? General Revari was our one hope of staying alive! Have you forgotten I helped her kill King Dubian? What do you think will happen to me once Queen Vivant finds out?"

Gallium continued placing the game pieces in order. "Brother, you're not looking at the big picture."

Dr. Barrios gripped his hair, tugging on it tightly. It was a habit he'd developed as a ChildForm. He'd never outgrown it.

Gallium snickered. "You're gonna go bald if you keep that up."

"Then maybe I'm an idiot, Gallium. Perhaps I don't see how *you* cannot see our impending death. Care to explain it to me as if I'm a ChildForm?"

"I thought you'd never ask, Dr. Barrios." He laughed at his brother's impatient sigh. "She didn't return with Queen Vivant. Neither did Major Legend or those six sexy pieces who enjoyed lying under Simonius."

One would never guess they were related. Dr. Barrios's large, bulbous nose and beady eyes starkly contrasted with Gallium's striking features. Dr. Barrios often wondered how his beautiful mother and handsome father ended up with a son as ugly as he.

"Now that tells me she didn't want to return to Platirius for one reason—she didn't want to serve under her sister," said Gallium. "We knew she'd never follow Queen Vivant's leadership."

Unnerved by Gallium's placidity, he took his hands out of his hair and knocked over a piece on the board. "I'm still not seeing what that has to do with us."

Gallium looked up at him. "She wants to rule a planet. If she can't have this one, she'll take another—the one she's on right now."

"Kikhani? You're not serious? Queen Aiki is crazier than her father was! She's beaten dozens of MaleForms who tried to overthrow her. What chance does she have of defeating her alone?"

"Think about it, Barrios. What does she have now that she didn't have when she tried to take over Earth?"

Confused, Dr. Barrios glanced curiously at Gallium. He'd just about lost all his patience. The Platirian dining staff had been ordered to give them half-portions of rations to keep them weakened. After being locked away for days, he was exhausted, hungry, and extremely irritable.

Gallium picked up on his silent cues and began explaining before Dr. Barrios lost focus. "Did you see how vigorous her son became holding King Dubian's BrainStaff? All General Revari has to do is conquer another planet and absorb it into Kikhani."

Dr. Barrios sat down. "Together, they'd be powerful enough to defeat Queen Vivant. The prophecy foretells that if Queen Vivant falls, the new ruler will come from Kikhani."

He began to see where Gallium was going. "I've known her since she was an InfantForm," said Gallium. "My guess is she tried to capture Queen Vivant in exchange for her freedom. When that didn't work, she set her sights on ruling Kikhani."

Dr. Barrios grimaced. Picturing General Revari becoming queen again scared him to death. "But what about Queen Aiki? She's not going to roll over and let General Revari and her son take her position."

"They won't have to take it from her. She's going to give it to them willingly."

Dr. Barrios cocked his head. "What are you getting at, Gallium?"

"King Hitam is still alive, but his father, grandfather, and many more kings died on Kikhani."

"So? The hybrid isn't of their bloodline."

"General Kron wasn't in King Dubian's bloodline, but was next in line to be king."

"Marriage? Are you suggesting the hybrid will marry her?"

Dr. Barrios snickered. "Gallium...Queen Vivant was—and is—a beautiful WomanForm! It was easy for General Kron to marry her. Any MaleForm would have been happy to align with her—even if it meant putting up with King Dubian's madness until he died."

Rubbing his bare arms to warm them against the chill of the confinement chamber, he said, "Queen Aiki is also easy on the eyes, but she's insane. She's gelded many of her opponents. No MaleForm in his right mind would marry her."

"She'd never allow a union between the two," said Gallium.

Gallium removed his coat and handed it to him. "He could easily trick Queen Aiki into believing he wants her. Once he helps General Revari take Kikhani, she'd be in a better position to challenge Queen Vivant for Platirius. With him by her side, she'll win."

Dr. Barrios gaped at Gallium. "What if he wants Kikhani or Platirius for himself?"

Gallium shook his head. "I've watched him closely. He won't betray her. He feels Queen Vivant cheated her out of ruling Platirius. He'll do whatever it takes to help his mother return to the top. That includes duping Queen Aiki into believing he wants to be her next king. Once her defenses are down, they'll kill her."

Gallium picked up the piece Dr. Barrios knocked over. "She may be pretty to you, but nothing is more seductive than power. Trust me when I say General Revari will become the next Queen of Kikhani. She's more skilled in battle than her son and knows the ins and outs of every kingdom in the galaxy."

Gallium sat looking down at the game board in satisfaction, then continued. "He knows nothing of how things operate outside of Earth. As more kings learn he exists, his inexperience will become a hindrance. She knows this."

He carefully studied his next move. "I think she'll use him to get what she wants and then ship him back to Earth. She won't risk allowing a solicitous king to kill him. Think of how she used the Human to get rid of Queen Vivant's daughters. Or how she used your knowledge as a physician to kill King Dubian."

"She used you too. To get Queen Vivant addicted to the CallePepper."

Gallium nodded solemnly. "It's what she does best. She moves MaleForms around like we've moved these pieces across the board all afternoon. King Dubian corrupted her mind against MaleForms."

His next move captured Dr. Barrios's strongest player on the board. "She uses us to her advantage, but she'll never trust us. That includes her son. It's just the way she is. Not even he will change her. He'll help her take Kikhani, but she'll never allow him to rule a planet on his own."

Dr. Barrios let out a long sigh. "You still haven't told me where we factor in to all this, little brother."

"I just told you. We're MaleForms, aren't we? She needs us on Kikhani to help her defeat the Kikhanians."

Dr. Barrios cleaned his glasses on his shirt. "There's just one problem with your theory. We're still on Platirius while she's on Kikhani. How long will it take before that nosy General Lyric comes busting in here demanding what we know?"

He bit his lip. "Queen Vivant has eschewed torture in the past, but if General Lyric starts whispering conspiracy theories in her ear, she'll have us tortured as sure as I'm sitting here!"

Gallium moved a game piece on the board. "It won't come to that."

Dr. Barrios eyed him suspiciously. "What do you know that I don't?"

Gallium smiled at him, genuinely pleased with himself. "I know many things, Ezra. She set her plans in motion years ago when she was locked away in the Chamber of Despair. For many nights, we sat and talked—planning her takeover."

Dr. Barrios opened his mouth, then closed it. Gallium didn't need to know what he'd done to make General Revari despise him. "She's covered every base, never neglected the slightest detail. The only thing she didn't see coming was her son and an unwanted trip to Kikhani. But none of that matters."

He watched Dr. Barrios make his move. "She's very good at taking the cards she's dealt and stacking them in her favor. She doesn't realize it now, but Queen Aiki has moved General Revari in a position to become Queen again. If we help her to accomplish her feat, we'll never have to worry about anyone killing us."

"You still haven't answered my question. What will stop us from being tortured and killed before we extend this help to her?"

Before Gallium could answer, both he and Dr. Barrios disappeared from the confinement chamber. Tentatively, Dr. Barrios opened his eyes and found himself looking up at General Revari and Prince Justin.

Gently punching his arm, Gallium grinned at him. "See? I told you."

"Welcome to Kikhani," said General Revari. "We hope you'll enjoy the accommodations."

"You have the gift of telepathy," breathed Dr. Barrios.

She looked down at him in disgust. "You may be a physician, but I've always said Gallium was smarter than you. I found a way to keep all of King Barron's energy after Platirius reunited."

Twisting her mouth scornfully, she said, "I call it severance pay for my sister stealing Platirius from me. Now, let's get to work. I've my sights set on the perfect planet to merge with Kikhani after I return from Earth."

Dr. Barrios and Gallium looked at each other. Things were about to get interesting.

General Lyric couldn't believe what she was hearing. "What do you mean they're gone?"

Sergeant Thea looked around the empty confinement chamber. "General Lyric, we had them under surveillance the whole time you and Queen Vivant were gone. They just disappeared right before our eyes. We have it on camera!"

General Lyric slapped her hands on her thighs. "I intended to interrogate Gallium on what he knows about General Revari. How am I supposed to do that now if they're not on Platirius?!"

"Is it possible the flagitious magic of Rubarius has transferred to General Revari?" asked Captain Kourtney.

"I don't know," admitted General Lyric glumly. "We were seldom allowed to enter Rubarius. General Revari didn't want us to know anything that went on over there. There's still so much mystery surrounding it. It was the only planet that disintegrated when Platirius became whole again."

She braced herself against a chair. "King Anemi acquired it and King Dubian inherited it. Both were the epitome of evil. I think that's what held Rubarius inside Platirius while they lived—the common threads of wickedness they and King Barron shared.

Folding her arms, General Lyric stared at the floor, thinking. "Maybe that's why Platirius split after King Dubian's death. The righteous half went to Queen Vivant, and General Revari inherited the evil realm. Maybe there was no other way the universe could do it."

Sergeant TamRi closed her eyes and sighed. "So, in a way, she's still the Queen of Rubarius."

"I'd say she is a living, breathing version of Rubarius," said General Lyric. "All the bloodshed on its grounds. The afflictions of the souls who lived under King Barron's reign—it's all inside her now."

The Vivacians looked around at each other. If what General Lyric suspected was true, then their troubles with General Revari were far from over.

Chapter 4

As Queen Aiki watched from a distance, General Revari lined up the impressive mass of Revaltians who had fled with Major Legend from Platirius. She'd also summoned all the Revaltians who had journeyed to Earth with her to Kikhani. Her army now stood facing the Kikhanians, waiting for her instructions.

"Major Legend, go and stand next to my son."

"Yes, General Revari."

She didn't speak again until the Major reached Prince Justin.

"It's time to separate the cream from the sour milk. Six of you were audacious enough to copulate with Simonius right under my nose. Let's see how brave you are now. Take a step forward. And so help me, if I have to weed you out, you'll experience more pain than you've ever felt in your lifespans."

Six soldiers took a tentative step toward her. "You ungrateful wenches. Who made you into the most powerful army in the galaxy? Who took you to heights you never would've reached had I not murdered King Dubian? Me!"

She walked down the row, looking each of them in the eye. "And you dared to lower yourselves to copulate with a filthy

MaleForm behind my back? After all the torment they've caused us?"

The guilty Revaltians trembled. They knew what was coming but were powerless to stop it.

"I freed you from the humiliation of having their feet on your necks. And how did you repay my kindness? You forfeited the honor of serving in my army for *Simonius*?"

She pursed her lips in distaste. "I had the unfortunate opportunity of seeing him unclothed during a torture session. Let me tell you, I wasn't impressed! Half a space worm is more well-endowed than he! You settled for *that*? Ridiculous!"

One of the soldiers burst into tears. "Queen Revari—I mean, General Revari—please let me explain!"

She faced the soldier. "You'd like to offer me an explanation? Did I hear that right?"

"Yes, General! Please. I still want to serve under you!"

She stared at her. "You allowed yourself to be sullied by a MaleForm. How did you think you'd still serve me after being on your back for him? Did you think you were smarter than I while you hid your wicked little trysts, soldier?"

The Revaltian shook her head. "No! I know I'm not smarter than you!"

She circled her like a panther over its kill. "Now you'll tell us...how much did Simonius see of you? Did you show him your body? Don't get quiet now, whore!"

The soldier, now terrified, wished she'd kept quiet. "Y—yes, I did."

She smiled. "Hmm... Did you show him your...tongue?"

"General? I'm so sorry!" she whined.

She glared at her. "I didn't ask if you were sorry. I asked if you showed him your tongue."

Now bawling, the soldier struggled to speak. "Yes, General Revari."

"Why are you crying now, soldier? You weren't crying when you were carrying on with him, right?"

She was too afraid to answer.

"RIGHT?" screamed General Revari.

"Right! Yes—I'm guilty!"

She pursed her lips. "The irony of you wanting to be a beacon of truth after months of using that nasty lying tongue of yours to pleasure Simonius. Let's see it. Let us all see the little tool that has landed you in so much trouble! Stick out your tongue."

The Revaltians shifted nervously. Their leader was as unpredictable as the weather. They had no idea what she was about to do. Queen Aiki, however, was enjoying the bit of entertainment. She sat forward in her seat in anticipation as the petrified soldier stuck out her tongue.

"Now you see it," said General Revari, elevating her voice. "Now you...DON'T!" With a single, fluid motion, she cut off the soldier's tongue. It fell to the ground, landing on top of her boot.

She screamed and held her hand to her mouth as blood gushed down her uniform. Gallium, Dr. Barrios, and Prince Justin sucked in their breath, but Queen Aiki laughed hysterically when the soldier fell to her knees.

"GET UP, YOU FILTHY WHORE! Hold her up!" commanded General Revari.

The soldiers grabbed her off the floor and stood her at attention. General Revari sliced deep into her belly, cutting upward from below her navel to between her breasts. She reached inside her, ripping through her intestines until they spilled out of her, before turning to the rest of the Revaltians, now paralyzed with fear.

"When I was married, my husband's family invited us to a pig roast in Cuba. I see I've lost some of you already. It's a place on Earth. Follow along and try to keep up with the lesson, Revaltians! I wish you could've seen all the pigs they slaughtered for us to eat. It was amazing! I think there were six or seven. I enjoyed watching all of them be gutted and cleaned."

Prince Justin looked at Major Legend before turning back to watch the unfolding bloody scene. She hadn't revealed this side of his birth mother. It was difficult to imagine growing up with her packing his lunches and attending games like Diana Colton, his adoptive mother, had.

She focused on the remaining Revaltians who'd betrayed her. "Then they salted them down and put them up on spits to roast. I still remember how they smelled. Absolutely incredible! Would you like to know something? That was the most delicious meat I'd ever had in my lifespan."

Terrified, her soldiers watched as she paced back and forth among them.

"Pigs place anything in their mouths, you know? And they lie in the mud rutting and grunting with other pigs. Now, when I think of dignified, the first animal that comes to mind isn't pigs. So what do you do with dirty pigs who place grimy things in their mouths?"

She methodically pointed her finger in the faces of the guilty Revaltians. "You *gut* them and toss them into the fire! Will the smell be as magnificent as the smell of roasted pork? Not to me." Placing one finger in the air, she said, "And yet...I learned a valuable lesson at that pig roast. Fire purifies all unclean things."

Dr. Barrios watched her terrorize the Revaltians. Unlike Gallium, he'd never been at ease around her. He hadn't realized he'd bitten his tongue until he noted the coppery taste of blood. It was a stark reminder to keep his secrets hidden from her.

"I intend to hold the title of queen again. Thanks to The One and my spoiled brat of a sister, I am now forced to rebrand my image. My army shall be pristine, honorable, and pure. I won't rebuild my empire on the backs of pigs who'll wallow in the mud with other pigs!"

She reached down, picked up an intestine, and rubbed it across the faces of the offenders. "Trust is hard to earn and so easy to lose. I have earned your trust through my actions and deeds. I will not accept less than what I give."

She held the intestine in the air. "Pigs...have no place among us. So here's what I'm going to do. I'm going to give you a choice. Choose to be gutted like sneaky little pigs and fed to the fire..."

Sensing their rising fear, she paused dramatically and waited. "Or you can be shipped back to Platirius and let my idiotic sister decide your fate. Who knows? Maybe she'll be in a forgiving mood."

She tapped her foot impatiently. "Either way, you are gravely mistaken if you think you'll get away with spitting on the honor of my reputation. I am the greatest warrior in the universe. No one betrays me without consequences."

Carefully scanning each of their faces, she said, "You have forgotten who I am," she said softly. "Now? I must make examples out of you." She tossed the intestine at the nearest guilty soldier. "How will it look to the galaxy if I surround myself with disrespectful pigs? Do you think it's fair to me to spare your lives?"

One of the soldiers made a move to strike General Revari with her sword, but before she could unsheathe it, her head rolled from her neck. Waves of anxiousness rippled through the Revaltians as she held her bloody sword extended away from her trim waist.

The Revaltian hadn't had time to think before she was cut down. General Revari picked up the head of the fallen soldier, holding it up for all to see. Prince Justin was astonished. He'd never witnessed such brutality.

"That's two down. Four to go. Do you see how copulating with MaleForms weakens your minds? Do you know why I forbade copulating with MaleForms? It strengthens *them*, not us!"

Blood dripped from the sword she pointed at them. "It makes you weak. And crazy. Just look! One thought she would talk her way out of her punishment, and another dared to raise her hand to me! Do you really think you have what it takes to kill me? Has a MaleForm sank your honor so low?"

She placed the head on top of her sword. "Would anyone else like to try and claim my head?"

No one moved.

Queen Aiki turned to Dr. Barrios. "I think she's enjoying herself. What do you think?"

Dr. Barrios looked at her out of the corner of his eye but didn't answer.

"Oh, she has you scared too, huh? A big, broad MaleForm like you? Tsk. Shameful."

Shut up, you...miscreant beast!

Dr. Barrios harrumphed and turned away from her. He stifled a cry when he felt her foot kick him hard in the behind. Despite watching a bloodbath, Gallium and Prince Justin struggled not to laugh at them.

A pinch from Major Legend silenced them. Clearing their throats, they redirected their attention back to the Revaltians. Queen Aiki, however, still glared at Dr. Barrios.

General Revari smiled at the soldiers. "Very well. Who wants to take a trip to Platirius?"

She waited. "No one? All right then...you've chosen the fate of pigs. You'll be gutted and placed on spits. Oh, I left out one little thing..."

Her targets withered under her malevolent scrutiny.

"Some of the Kikhanians"—she turned to look at them before returning to the four soldiers standing at attention—"are cannibals. Now, Queen Vivant would've sent you into the sun, but since we're guests on Kikhani, I'll be the founder of their first feast. Consider yourselves dishonorably discharged from the Revaltians."

Ignoring their loud protests, she announced, "They're all yours."

With a triumphant roar, a group of Kikhanians seized the expelled WomenForms and collected the two that lay dead on the ground. Lifting them in the air, they chanted a war song while carrying them to the other side of the mountain.

Queen Aiki whispered in Dr. Barrios's ear. "You're plump enough to eat too, you know?"

Gallium tried not to wince as Dr. Barrios grabbed his wrist, squeezing hard. Prince Justin closed his eyes to avoid laughing again.

General Revari met Major Legend's eyes but addressed an up-and-coming Revaltian. "Corporal Kiki, I'm assigning you to shadow under Captain Angela. Queen Aiki has agreed to allow us to stay while I assist her with a mission. Stay with her and learn the ropes. I have my eye on some of you for promotions."

Saluting her fearless leader, she said, "Thank you, General. I'm looking forward to proving myself."

General Revari's silver eyes assessed her. "You already have. You collected the most souls for Earth's absorption. It hasn't gone unnoticed."

Corporal Kiki was rewarded with rounds of applause and good-natured ribbing from her teammates.

General Revari turned to Captain Angela. "Make sure everyone chooses a room and prepares for supper, but let me warn you—don't eat any meat you're unsure of."

She laughed and saluted her. "I'll take care of everything. It's good to have her back, isn't it, Revaltians?"

The Revaltians loudly cheered and hooted.

She smiled at the WomenForms who had laid their lives on the line to rescue her. "It's good to be back. Major Legend? I'd like to speak with you privately. Queen Aiki, can we use your meeting chambers?"

"Oh, of course, General Revari. I don't eat Platirians, but I'd like to see how they'll be prepared. Some of my warriors come up with the most unique ideas." She got up to follow the Kikhanians.

"Prince Justin, Gallium, and Dr. Barrios, you'll stay on the opposite side of the palace. MaleForms don't bunk with or eat with WomenForms."

Dr. Barrios sighed with relief, and Prince Justin said, "Yeah, General Lyric told us before we came to get you, Mama."

She raised an eyebrow. "General Lyric? When did she have the chance to speak to you?"

"Right after I threatened to cut off Queen Vivant's head."

She chuckled. *That's my boy.*

"Gallium?" She handed him her bloody sword. "There's no one I trust more to handle this than you."

He tested its weight and smiled. "I remember the day your Grandfather, King Carlomon, gifted this to your mother. She'd just been appointed general."

His sea-green eyes held hers. "She would've been so proud of you."

She looked away for a moment. "You're all I have of her. Thank you, Gallium. You know how much that means to me."

His breath caught at the sheen of tears that gathered in her eyes. In a flash, they were gone, replaced by her usual icy facade.

So, the iron-hard general can be vulnerable, huh?

Had he not seen it with his own eyes, he wouldn't have believed it.

"Did she teach you how to fight?" asked Prince Justin.

She smiled sadly. "No. Gallium did."

Startled, he looked from her to Gallium, but neither elaborated. He felt the waves of pain flowing within her.

What was the connection between her and the handsome man at her side?

"Go with Gallium and Dr. Barrios. Major Legend? Come with me."

P rince Justin followed them until they almost reached the palace before placing a hand on Gallium's arm. Dr. Barrios hurried inside the palace. The day's events fueled an eagerness for a good meal and a reprieve from General Revari's antics.

"Did my Grandmother raise her to be that tough?"

Gallium assessed him for a moment before answering. "No. Queen Dellah died giving birth to her."

He noted the prince's stunned expression but kept silent.

"You had to have been a kid when it happened, right?"

"I'm the same age I was when I watched her die," said Gallium coolly.

"How can that be when you look younger than I am? I wouldn't have guessed you were older than twenty. It defies scientific explanation!"

Gallium's eyes narrowed into slits. "It defies *Human* logic—your limited perception of science. I hate to break it to you, but Humans aren't the standard for the rest of Space. You're not average either. I'd say a million levels below average sums you up perfectly. We could fill a pocket of Space with what your finite minds don't understand."

He stilled at his discourteous tone. "You hate us. Have you always been this bitter?"

It was impossible to read the Alien's expression. "That's no secret, but as General Revari's son, you're the exception. I could no more hate a part of her than I could hate myself. As for the second part of your statement, if I'm bitter, your Grandfather introduced me to it—many times over."

He should've been put off by Gallium's acerbic nature, but he wasn't. For reasons he couldn't explain, he felt Gallium was a decent soul. Apparently, there was a lot to unravel about his mother's side of the family.

"Unless you have more questions, Your Highness, we should get ready for supper."

He stuck his hand out to him. "Listen, none of that *Your Highness* nonsense, all right? Just call me Justin."

Gallium looked at the hand, then shook it firmly. As he followed him into the palace, he wondered what his mother and Major Legend were discussing. He hoped she'd go easy on his aunt.

She'd been a second mother to him, and a damned fine one. He hoped that would be enough to quench General Revari's thirst for revenge.

S hakily, Major Legend followed Revari into Queen Aiki's spacious den. To her disgust, it was filled with books about cannibalism and copulation—two prized subjects on Kikhani.

General Revari sat down across from her. "You have five seconds to tell me why I shouldn't feed you to the Kikhanians. Don't even think of using my son to save your skin. You had no right to keep him from me!"

Major Legend sighed. The moment of truth had finally come. Whatever she said now would save or lose her life. "I took Prince Justin so he wouldn't die. I tried to save your husband too, but King Dubian never assigned me the task of watching over him for long."

Major Legend's voice was barely above a whisper as she recalled bitter memories from the past. "He ordered Corporal Fontine and the other MaleForms to...torture him. I brought him water whenever I could. King Dubian ordered me to inject him with Ashion every three hours."

General Revari clenched her fist so tightly, her nails sank into her palm. Ashion wouldn't kill Humans, but it triggered terrifying hallucinations.

Before fleeing Platirius, some of the Humans she had experimented on had pounded their heads on the walls or clawed their own eyes out. She wished she could reclaim King Dubian's body and kill him again.

"But I couldn't do it. I didn't want to increase his suffering. So I replaced the Ashion with liquid nourishment and told him to pretend he was under its influence. It broke my heart when he kept asking about you. He never thought of himself—only of you. I knew I had to keep him alive until I could find a way to help you escape."

She wiped tears from her eyes and shuddered. "But it was too late. By the time I helped you escape, he was dying. I wanted you to see him...one last time."

"Why did you care whether or not Oliver and I escaped from Platirius? And why did you take my baby?"

"I'm not sorry I did it," she admitted. "If I could go back in time, I wouldn't change anything. You mean much more to me than you know. You always have."

She held General Revari's eyes. "I'm your half-sister. King Dubian was my father too."

Queen Vivant had a secret. She had been careful to uphold the image of the cool, calm, and decisive leader she'd been before becoming addicted to Callidut. It was a lie. She was finally the sole Queen of Platirius, but her mounting troubles nearly overwhelmed her.

It was a daily struggle not to succumb to her cravings. Opening the door of her daughters' bed chamber, she stood looking around the expansive space.

Her eyes were drawn to a row of three spacious beds covered with different styles of bedding, fluffy pillows, dolls, and soft toys. She picked up Princess Teenah's favorite stuffed animal and took its place on the bed.

She lay down, holding it close to her heart. The sweet, sugary scent of the toy brought memories of her daughters flooding to her mind.

Echoes of their laughter filled the bed chamber. She'd purposely stayed away from places she expected to see them for many reasons.

Now that Platirius was whole again, she was responsible for bringing order to all the daily activities in her queendom. Although the numerous tasks were never-ending, she couldn't keep herself busy enough to stop missing them.

Restoring order to her army was the first priority. The Revaltians had no place on Platirius—there was only one army now. All soldiers who had served under General Revari were either on Earth or Kikhani. Any Revaltian uniforms and miniature TeleScreens left behind were collected and burned.

She wanted to be prepared when the time came to defend Platirius from its enemies. Kikhani was at the top of that list. If Queen Aiki had allowed them to leave so easily, it meant she had bigger plans—unfortunately, plans that now involved General Revari. It was an unlikely and deadly union.

She knew her sister despised the Kikhanians and the feeling was mutual. She suspected General Revari hadn't gone to Kikhani willingly. If she had been a prisoner initially, clearly that was no longer the case.

What could they possibly have in common that would inspire them to join forces?

She never actually believed General Revari would return with her. It was a silly dream to hope she'd help her rebuild Platirius. She'd expected her to return to Earth, cooling her heels until she devised her next plan to claim her throne. Now she was on Kikhani.

She feared General Revari reuniting with her son might cause its own set of problems. MaleForms were hated and feared on every planet run by WomenForms. She'd witnessed how the Kikhanians had responded to Prince Justin. They wanted him gone.

Only Queen Aiki seemed to accept his presence. She blatantly loved copulating with MaleForms. Rumor had it she'd lain with two or three MaleForm prisoners in a single night.

Trying to probe her mind hadn't assisted her in uncovering the truth. She was insane. Her mind—a mass of disorganized thoughts—proved to be useless when she scanned it.

Hoping to scare her into allowing her to take the Revaltian soldiers, she'd lied to her. Without anyone left to teach her how to rule Kikhani, she had no knowledge of how to run a successful queendom. And so, she was easily deceived.

Thanks to her, the Kikhanians would remain wary of Prince Justin. She hoped the seed she planted would cause them to make them leave. Unlike Platirius, copulation on Kikhani didn't empower MaleForms.

Beyond Platirius, copulation had no effect at all on either SexForm. Once, King Hitam and Queen Amori had been deeply in love. Together, they ushered Kikhani into a kingdom more impressive than that of his predecessors.

But millions of years later, King Hitam became dispassionate. Like many kings, he frequently took trips to other planets, including Earth. After returning home, he had disclosed to his wife that he'd fallen in love with a Human woman. He renounced his authority on Kikhani and left for Earth.

Queen Amori was so devastated, she had taken her own life in front of their daughter. That was the beginning of her madness. She wanted love and affection from MaleForms, yet she took great pleasure in killing them after promising to make them her king.

Her sporadic mind changed frequently. One could never trust what she said. After she murdered a third prince from a neighboring planet, royal MaleForms refused to accept invitations to marry her.

Heaven forbid one lost in a battle to her. It didn't matter whether she found him pleasing to the eyes. After she finished slaking her lust, he was as good as dead. She blamed King Hitam for her mother's death and enjoyed unleashing years of suppressed rage on her victims.

She wouldn't waste any time setting her sights on General Revari's son, which would prove to be the biggest mistake of her lifespan.

She saw how enthralled her sister was with him. She'd cut Queen Aiki's head off twice if she dared to raise a hand to him. He was too green to hold his own against her and the Kikhanians.

Even with General Revari's impressive number of soldiers, without a BrainStaff, he was powerless to fight off an attack. And that...was another reason for her to leave Kikhani.

Why had she remained?

Chapter 5

Queen Vivant sat up and returned the toy to its place. Two
MaleForms who had worked closely with General Revari
were still on Platirius. She was interested in speaking with the
one they called Gallium.

Dr. Barrios had been a trusted advisor to King Dubian.
Although neither she or General Revari had liked him, his
services were needed after King Dubian died.

Gallium was a different story. Before General Revari was born,
she'd shared an amicable relationship with him. But as the years
passed, her bond with him had grown cold and distant. The
acrimonious feud between him, her husband, and her father had
made it impossible for things to continue as they were.

Her father's death had been the catalyst for planting the final
nail in the coffin. Swearing allegiance solely to the throne of
Rubarius, he had become her sister's protector and confidant.
She hadn't been surprised when General Revari vehemently
opposed him joining the Mass Deaths.

If anyone had intimate knowledge of her plans, it would be
him. She knew how her daughters had died, but she didn't know
why. That bothered her the most. Guilt washed over her as she

struggled to make sense of why someone would want to use her ChildForms to hurt her.

Now that her mind was clear of the Callidut, she realized the Human had merely been a pawn in someone's game. Since he wasn't the mastermind, the real killer was still out there. She couldn't bring herself to suspect her sister.

Yes, General Revari was ruthless, but she'd always had a soft spot for ChildForms. Maybe General Lyric's intense dislike of her was clouding her judgment. She looked around the bed chamber again, willing her anxiety to lessen.

She hadn't allowed the cleaning staff to remove the princesses' belongings. Everything looked exactly as it did on the day of their last LifeCelebration. Leaning against the door, she suppressed a fresh round of tears. Her heart felt as if it'd been shredded into pieces. In time, she'd avenge her daughters' deaths. But for the moment, she wanted to see Gallium.

General Lyric and Sergeant Thea met her at the entrance of the confinement chamber. "Your Highness, Gallium and Dr. Barrios have disappeared," said General Lyric.

Queen Vivant cocked her head. "Well, that confirms it, doesn't it?"

"Confirms what, My Queen?" asked Sergeant Thea.

"My sister and Queen Aiki are working on something big. Otherwise, why would they need Gallium on Kikhani?"

She looked around at the empty confinement chamber and saw a game sitting on a small table. Closely observing the board, she took note of each detail. All the pieces except for two were in perfect alignment. As she stared at the board, she realized what Queen Aiki wanted with General Revari.

She turned to General Lyric and Sergeant Thea with a satisfied smile. "I know what they're going to do."

"What?" asked Sergeant Thea.

"You were able to probe her mind?" asked General Lyric. "Some of our best magicians have described her mind as a war zone."

"It is, but I didn't learn anything by scanning her mind. Someone else told me what she plans to do—Gallium."

Confused, General Lyric and Sergeant Thea looked at each other. She picked up the two pieces that faced each other and held them up in the air. "They're going after the King of Kikhani. Queen Aiki wants to kill him, and she's enlisted General Revari to help her do it."

"But they hate each other," said Sergeant Thea. "Why would General Revari help her?"

She pursed her lips. "Queen Aiki hasn't been in the game as long as Platirians have. She's so focused on repaying her father for what happened to her mother that she doesn't realize that once General Revari kills him, she will become the new head of Kikhani."

"But he's on Earth," said Sergeant Thea. "He hasn't led Kikhani for hundreds of years. That's a long time to wait for revenge."

General Lyric stared at the two game pieces before looking up at Queen Vivant. "She's going to kill Queen Aiki too!"

"Of course she will. Killing is what she does best. That's why Queen Aiki wants her. That's only one part of the plan. My sister has probably told her she'd have to help her fight me for Platirius."

"But if she kills King Hitam, she won't need her. His power will transfer to her instead of Queen Aiki," said General Lyric.

Queen Vivant set the pieces down on the board. "Yes, but Queen Aiki doesn't know that. General Revari and I watched our father and my husband lead Platirius. We learned how to deal with enemies and barter and trade with other realms to stimulate our economy."

The queen's silver eyes took in every detail of the confinement chamber, remembering a few of the souls that had been housed there. "King Hitam left when she was a ChildForm. She had no one to study and learn the way of things. She's been leading Kikhani out of instinct and impulsivity, and it's worked...until now."

Captain Kourtney entered the confinement chamber. "I think I can guess the topic of discussion—General Revari."

Without waiting for an answer, she lifted the fallen chairs and rearranged them at the table.

"You would be correct, Captain Kourtney," said Queen Vivant. "Two things are working against her. She's ended the lives of many prominent MaleForms and has allowed some of her subjects to indulge in cannibalism—a disgusting practice."

The queen grimaced. "Her actions have alienated her from most of the galaxy. No Being wants to enter into any form of agreement with Kikhani."

General Lyric, Captain Kourtney, and Sergeant Thea listened as they tidied up the confinement chamber.

"Had King Hitam remained on Kikhani until the end of his lifespan, his essence would've gone into its grounds and energized it for years."

Queen Vivant returned the game pieces to a chrome box and set it on a high shelf. "Since he left, she's been stealing Beings from all over to keep her planet fully powered. If she committed the murder herself, she wouldn't have to worry about seeking new sources of energy. Also, his knowledge and power would go to her."

"But she's had years to take out King Hitam," said Sergeant Thea. "Why hasn't she?"

"She's not skilled enough to end him," said Queen Vivant. "But General Revari is. Queen Aiki seldom fights in battles—only her warriors. When General Revari fought under General Kron, she learned many of his techniques."

Remembering how much she'd loved her husband made her smile. "Lucian died undefeated in battle. She doesn't realize she's set General Revari up to receive all of Kikhani's power and take it over. Once that's done, where do you think she'll come next?"

"Here," said Captain Kourtney. "She'll come for Platirius."

"Correct. As the new leader of Kikhani, she'll challenge me to claim Platirius. It will happen just as the Surveyors prophesied it would."

"Then Queen Aiki has just slit her own throat," said General Lyric.

Queen Vivant nodded. "Oh yes. She's about to discover my sister's blade is never dull."

General Revari poured two drinks before handing one to Major Legend. "What do you mean King Dubian was your father?"

"He didn't always look down his nose at commoners. His parents, King Anemi and Queen Zherta, despised him because King Anemi had an affair with his mother."

Major Legend stuffed plush pillows behind her back, making herself comfortable in the oversized chair. "When he was a ChildForm, making friends was very important to him. It didn't matter who as long as they showed him the attention he craved. My mother was his first friend."

She stopped short of accepting the drink General Revari handed to her. "If you think I'd kill you before discovering what you know, then you never knew me." The two WomenForms stared at each other. One was calm and the other feared for her life. Major Legend tentatively accepted the cup.

"They played together from dawn until dusk. At that time, my mother was very young—just transitioning from a ChildForm to a junior WomanForm. She was naive enough to become fond of him and left flowers for him in secret places around the palace."

Major Legend's eyes formed into slits. "Once he laid eyes on your mother, he changed. He grew cold and haughty, believing anyone who wasn't royalty was beneath him."

She took a drink before continuing. "He told my mother they were no longer friends. She was crushed. She left flowers for him, hoping to rekindle their friendship, but he flew into a rage when he discovered it was she who had been giving him flowers instead of Princess Dellah."

The soft light of the candles cast shadows against the walls of the meeting chamber. Major Legend's lip quivered as she struggled to conceal the emotions she'd suppressed most of her life. General Revari patiently waited for her to compose herself.

"He beat her mercilessly," she whispered. "Then...he forced himself on her."

General Revari briefly closed her eyes. She had always known how atrocious her father was, but discovering he'd violated Major Legend's mother only intensified her hatred of him.

"My mother was a virgin. She had no knowledge of copulation with a MaleForm. He didn't care. He made the act as humiliating and painful as he could for her. Then, when he finished, he spit on her. Right in her face. She gathered up her clothes and ran from him."

Holding out the cup for more, she waited until it was full. "Out of fear he'd try to harm her again, she returned to Coldarius. After some time had passed, she realized she was carrying me. Had he discovered I was created during the violation, he would've killed her."

The Kikhanians' low, fast-paced chanting flowed through the walls of the palace and high up into Space.

"My grandparents were good people. Instead of shaming her, they helped her conceal the pregnancy. They told the neighbors they adopted me once I was born."

She looked up at General Revari. "Many years later, she met my father. They fell in love and he promised her he would rear me as his own."

She smiled to herself. "He was a gardener, like Gallium. He earned a lot of landscaping bids for other royal families, so he traveled a lot. Before King Dubian betrayed King Carlomon, Platirius and Coldarius had an amicable relationship. There was free movement between the planets."

General Revari poured herself another drink. It now made sense why she and Queen Vivant had been unable to probe Major Legend's mind—they shared King Dubian's blood. When he decreed the sisters wouldn't be permitted to penetrate each other's thoughts, he'd unknowingly included her.

"I don't remember much about my father, but he was very kind to Mother and I. The first time I met King Dubian, he visited our flower shop. I was shocked that I could read his mind. I felt the evilness within him—heavy and suffocating. After he left, she told me he was my real father. There was no way I'd reveal her secret."

"So, my MotherForm became your SecondMother," said General Revari.

"Yes, but I never thought of her that way. She was so kind and good. I held nothing but respect for Queen Dellah. I always will."

A knock at the door interrupted them. It was Lieutenant Sheila.

"General, I brought supper for you and Major Legend. We cooked the beef so there wouldn't be any mix-up with eating the...traitors." She shuddered and set the tray down before the WomenForms.

General Revari looked over the medium-well steaks, baked potatoes with all the trimmings, and vegetable salad. There were also small dishes of peach pie—General Revari's favorite—and vanilla ice cream. She smiled up at her.

"Thank you, Lieutenant Sheila. I'm happy to see all of you again. I'm looking forward to promoting you and Captain Angela once I reclaim my throne."

The lieutenant smiled at her. "We're happy to see you too. We hated being on Platirius without you."

"I trust the protective shield I placed on your minds worked?" asked General Revari. "No doubt Queen Vivant tried to learn our secrets once she recovered from the Callidut."

Lieutenant Sheila winked at her. "I overheard her talking to General Lyric on the WarCraft. She was irritated she couldn't read our minds."

General Revari grinned at her.

Bowing to her, she left them to continue their journey into the past.

"This looks delicious. It's nice to see many of my Revaltians are still loyal to me."

Major Legend sliced into the thick ribeye. "And we always will be. She's one of our best soldiers. Now, what was I saying? Oh! I was raised in a happy home with loving parents. My FatherForm passed when I was four, and I helped my MotherForm operate her flower shop."

She took a bite of the tender meat and chewed. "I never wanted for anything. There was always enough to eat and plenty of love to go around. My MotherForm, along with billions of Coldarians, was murdered."

She shuddered as if reliving the fate of the Coldarians she'd grown up with. "I had already enlisted in Coldarius's army, so when Queen Opal married King Dubian, many Coldarian soldiers were brought to Platirius to serve under them."

Accepting a large spoonful of sour cream, she said, "Being a soldier saved me. It also gave me an advantage in learning everything I could about him and his family."

Major Legend passed a small bowl of crispy shallots to General Revari. "He wasn't well-liked, but was tolerated due to Queen

Dellah's popularity. But after she died, he was positively loathed. He took his grief out on everyone. Especially you."

General Revari peeked underneath the dessert tray and smiled.

"I saw how much he loved Princess Vivant and how awful he was to you," said Major Legend. "I remember the first time I saw you. The way he treated you angered me. I saw parts of myself in you."

Major Legend furiously sliced into the steak again. "I expected you to be cold and distant like Princess Vivant, but you weren't. You treated the soldiers as if we mattered to you."

She smiled at General Revari. "You didn't look down your nose at us or expect us to cater to your every whim like Princess Vivant. I vowed to do what I could to protect you against him, but being a WomanForm in those times meant you had no power."

She placed a large pat of butter into her potato. "Gallium and I grew up in Coldarius. He'd come to Platirius with Princess Dellah before she married King Dubian. We lost our families in the freeze, so we share a mutual hatred of King Dubian. And we both wanted to bring as much joy as possible into your life."

She wiped her hand over her eyes. "But we failed to shield you from his cruelty. You grew up to be angry and distrustful. Even though I missed you, I was so proud of you for running away from Platirius."

She poured a bit of dressing on her salad. "Gallium and I hoped you'd found happiness and would never return. Then, before we knew it, you were back on Platirius with your husband and his family."

She looked into General Revari's eyes again. "Your husband's sister revealed where you were. It wasn't his parents. She made a deal with King Dubian not to harm your husband or their parents in exchange for you."

She frowned, removing the tomatoes from the salad. She hated tomatoes. "Of course, King Dubian lied to her. He wanted to hurt Oliver the most because you loved him. It killed him to see you being so warm with a Human when you'd never extended any amicable feelings toward him."

General Revari took her tomatoes and added them to her plate, taking careful note of what she'd learned. She had assumed it was Oliver's parents who had betrayed her—that was the reason she despised Humans. Were it not for Miguel and Benita Ascencio, Oliver would've never existed, and she wouldn't have met him and fallen in love.

Now she knew they hadn't. Faithful to her to the end, they had also met a senseless death. She listened as Major Legend's clear, strong voice drowned out the noise buzzing outside of Queen Aiki's palace.

"He was crazy to think you'd care for him when he'd never given you any reason to! He ordered the parents to be killed first. Then...he let the MaleForm soldiers have their way with the sister."

Major Legend's eyes started tearing up again. "The things they did to her were abominable. King Dubian wanted to make sure he stripped her of every bit of dignity before she died, and he succeeded."

She dried her eyes. "I couldn't let him hurt your InfantForm. General Kron was on a mission to discover who broke you out of the confinement chamber and provided the uniform for your husband."

So that's how the uniform got there, thought General Revari. She suspected Major Legend had hidden it, yet she wasn't sure.

"I set up Corporal Sinwalt to take the fall. King Dubian didn't give him a chance to defend himself. While they executed him, I switched your baby with that of a WomanForm who worked in the research chamber."

Now I finally know whose InfantForm I held before King Dubian took it away.

"She worked through her pregnancy, being exposed to various chemicals, so the baby never had a chance of surviving. She didn't care about it. She left him alone in the medical chamber, waiting to die. I took him and switched him with Prince Justin. Then I took him to Earth."

"Why Earth?" asked General Revari. "Why take my baby to that godforsaken place?"

"Because had he remained on Platirius or even another planet, his powers would've matured with him. He wouldn't have been able to hide that he was a royal."

"And that would've made him a target," finished General Revari. "Not only for King Dubian, but other kings would have tried to kill him too."

She sighed. "And he's still in the same predicament. He knows nothing of our ways. By now, news has traveled about a hybrid heir living among us. Kings from all over will want to eliminate him as a rival for Platirius's throne. I won't allow anyone to kill my son."

"Neither will I. He's my nephew. I've always looked out for him, the way I tried to protect you. And I always will."

"I have another sister," said General Revari in amazement.

"Yes, you do—a sister who loves you and is dedicated to seeing you finally get all the happiness you deserve. I know I made a terrible mistake copulating with Simonius. I didn't want him. I was reacting out of hurt when I turned to Simonius."

General Revari lifted a brow. "Explain."

"Well, when Gallium rejected my advances, it made me angry."

Puzzled, General Revari stopped chewing. "Gallium? You tried to copulate with Gallium? Why?"

"I've been in love with Gallium for a long time. He loves me too. Had we remained on Coldarius, we would've been married by now. But you and Queen Vivant changed Platirius's laws after you killed King Dubian. We couldn't be together."

She couldn't recall a time when she'd seen General Revari speechless. "Gallium's loyalty to you is unshakable. He's faithfully taken the *Quinite* he created to suppress his urges, while I became so busy that I neglected to. I know it's no excuse, but that's why I had a momentary lapse in judgment."

Major Legend frowned. "I was only with Simonius once, but that was enough. When I confessed what I'd done to Gallium, he was so angry with me."

Her voice trailed off. "But in time...he forgave me. He forced me to start retaking *Quinite*, and I haven't missed a dose. I don't want to disappoint him again. Or you."

She realized, unlike Queen Vivant, Major Legend had consistently shown loyalty to her over the years. General Revari had enjoyed the look on Queen Vivant's face when she informed her it was Major Legend who saved her son from her and King Dubian.

Fully aware that her eldest sister was jealous of the bond she shared with Major Legend, it pleased her to provoke Queen Vivant whenever the opportunity arose.

"If you'll forgive me, I promise never to fail you again."

General Revari noted the sincerity in her eyes. "I won't kill you," she said. "Not because of everything you did to save my baby and Oliver. You've just revealed you're my sister. Lying with Simonius pales in comparison to what Queen Vivant did to me. You tried to undo what she and King Dubian set in motion."

Beginning to see Major Legend in a new light, she said, "And...when I look back, you've always been there for me. That's something my other sister will never be able to say. Because of you, I have a living piece of my husband."

General Revari shook her head in wonderment. "I never thought I'd be able to look into his eyes again. One slip-up doesn't erase all the years of loyalty you've given me. I never knew how much King Dubian made you suffer until now."

The general's hand clenched into a fist. "I say we both deserve vengeance."

Major Legend's body shook as she continued weeping in front of her.

General Revari frowned at her. "Do that on your time. As of now, I'm appointing you to Colonel. I need you and Gallium to help me take Kikhani."

Colonel Legend dried her eyes again and smiled. "You know we will. I can't believe Queen Aiki doesn't know she's given you the keys to her queendom."

"She's too green. Her father didn't stick around to teach her the ropes. I've learned Kikhani has different rules. It was built on love before King Hitam turned his back on it and let his crazy daughter almost ruin it. None of the madness of my ancestors is in its grounds."

General Revari stood up and stretched her legs. "And I finally understand a bit more about Coldarius. Gallium always looked so wounded when someone mentioned it, I never asked about his home."

Colonel Legend nodded. She knew exactly how Gallium felt.

"If you and he came together, it wouldn't twist his mind against you like Platirian MaleForms," said General Revari.

"You and he could finally be together—if it's what you both wanted."

Chapter 6

C olonel Legend stared at her in astonishment. "I can't
believe what I'm hearing."

General Revari pushed away her supper plate and retrieved the
little dish that held a generous slice of pie. "Legend, my chance
at love was taken away from me. I can tell you that being away
from the ghosts of Platirius changes your way of thinking."

She took a bite of the pie, savoring its sweet spiciness. "I'd
never follow King Dubian's footsteps and deny you and Gallium
the chance to love each other off of Platirius. What justification
would I have?"

Adding a generous dollop of whipped cream to the pie, she
said, "My sister may have her head in the sand believing Platirius
is pure and wholesome now that she's running things, but I
know better."

She dug into the pie again. "Platirius still bears the souls of
King Dubian, King Anemi, and all the other oppressive, twisted
kings who built it. For us to thrive, we had to rid it of MaleForms.
But it's a new atmosphere on Kikhani. It was built with love, not
despotism."

She paused, reflecting on what she'd learned about Kikhani and what it could mean for the future. "Since we're not bound by evil spirits anymore, we all have a chance to start over. Well...as soon as I clear out Queen Aiki and the rest of her crazy clan."

"I know you're not big on touch, but there's something I've always wanted to do."

General Revari looked up from her plate. "What's that?"

Colonel Legend got up and walked over to where General Revari sat. Carefully, she kneeled and wrapped her arms around her. Suddenly, flashes of memories filled her mind.

She saw a young Colonel Legend and Gallium holding hands and eating ice cream. Gallium smiling up at Queen Dellah in the middle of a grand garden, and Colonel Legend playing with an infant Prince Justin. She laughed when she saw Colonel Legend spit in King Dubian's food and toss Queen Vivant's favorite scarf in a commode.

Finally allowing herself to be open to the promise of a new, brighter future, she returned her sister's embrace. She had only wanted to sit on the throne out of spite for King Dubian. But he was long dead. Now that she had her son, there was no need to prove her worth to a ghost.

A part of her family—ones he would've stopped at nothing to eliminate—was with her on Kikhani. Learning her son was alive and that she had a new sister freed some of the past bonds that had held her down for so many years.

Still, one person wasn't by her side—the one she missed the most. Oliver. Queen Vivant wouldn't get away with playing her part in his death. More than ever, she was determined to make her pay.

Acquiring more power and making new memories awaited her in the future. If she couldn't experience love for herself, she'd watch it proliferate in the lives of others—Colonel Legend and Gallium. And if her son chose a suitable bride. Of course, not Queen Aiki, and definitely not that idiotic General Lyric.

General Revari, finally freed of King Dubian's withering intolerance, felt more alive than she had in years. She was ready to embrace her new future. But first...she needed to get rid of King Hitam and his oddball daughter.

Gallium proved to be more resistant to the new change General Revari wanted to implement once she took over Kikhani. He looked up from his work at the WomenForms standing before him. His sea-green gaze bounced from Colonel Legend to her before returning to Colonel Legend.

"I don't think so," he told her.

"Gallium, things will be different for us now," said Colonel Legend. "She just explained why we couldn't be together on Platirius, but we don't have to worry about that anymore! Life on Kikhani will be a whole new experience for us."

Silently, he observed General Revari. Both WomenForms could tell he didn't believe a word she'd said.

General Revari hunkered down in front of him. "Gallium, do you really think I'd kill you?"

"Yes," he said without hesitation.

Surprised, she stared at him. "Have I ever given you a reason to think I'd want you gone?"

He shrugged. "Not me personally, but I know you don't like MaleForms. King Dubian didn't make it easy for you to care about us. In fact, I think he's the reason you find it so easy to kill us."

"That's true, but I fell in love with a male and gave birth to one. You shielded me from many things as a ChildForm. You were my first true friend. I've never forgotten how kind you were to me, Gallium. I have no more desire to hurt you than I would my own son."

"But I'm not your son. I'm an unrelated MaleForm."

She wanted to hit him. "How can you say that with a straight face? You've treated me as a daughter more than my own father. And...you wouldn't be unrelated if you married my sister."

He blinked. "I'd do anything for you, but I don't like Queen Vivant."

To his amazement, she laughed. Over the years, he had seldom witnessed her laughing. "I don't mean Queen Vivant. I mean my other sister, Colonel Legend. King Dubian was her father too."

He stared at Colonel Legend as if he'd never seen her before.

Observing his speechlessness, Colonel Legend said, "I'll fill you in if you stop being so knuckleheaded."

He shook his head furiously. "Legend, we can't be together. We'll be killed."

Colonel Legend gently shook him by the shoulders. "She just told you copulation isn't forbidden here, silly! Will you listen?"

Patiently, she explained everything she'd shared with General Revari. He took in every detail of her face. To him, she didn't look like King Dubian or the queens.

"I—can't believe it! All this time, you knew you were his daughter, but you never told me?"

She dropped her head. "I didn't know how you'd feel about it. I didn't want you to hate me."

He set aside the CallePepper plant he was working on. "I suspected something was off when I heard Queen Vivant complaining she couldn't read your mind."

He shook his head in amazement. "The whole time you were half Platirian—and a royal!"

His pretty eyes roamed over her again, making heat pool between Colonel Legend's thighs. "King Dubian announced the sisters wouldn't be able to read each other's minds after his subjects turned on him for using General Revari's *nued* points to find her. He never lived that down."

His gaze traveled from General Revari to the WomanForm he'd loved most of this life. "I never would've guessed you were related. I just thought you wanted to protect General Revari because you had a good heart."

She stroked his beard. "That much is true. I would've done it out of love, even if she wasn't my sister. You told me you wouldn't hold what I did with Simonius against me."

Glancing at General Revari, he cleared his throat. "Uh, Legend, we don't have to talk about that right now."

"Do you really forgive her?" asked General Revari.

"Of course I do. I probably would've done the same thing if it weren't for the Quinite. Copulation wasn't prohibited on Coldarius, so I know how it feels to be weak. I haven't held it against her. Simonius was a snake, but Legend is worth her weight in gold."

As if embarrassed by what he'd just revealed, he coughed and looked around. "Well, I'd better get back to making more Callidut if we're going to use it on the Kikhanians." He felt the general's eyes on him. Tentatively, he turned around to face her again.

"I don't know why you've remained loyal to me, but it won't go unrewarded. If it takes the rest of my lifespan, I will repay you for protecting me when I was a ChildForm. But...don't break my sister's heart," General Revari warned.

Alarmed, he looked from her to Colonel Legend and back to her again. "There's no need for repayment. When you were born, I promised Queen Dellah I'd keep you safe. Even though you're a WomanForm now, I'll always keep my promise to her."

His eyes clouded with sadness. "She's been gone a long time now, but I've kept her memory alive by being there for you. She was my friend. As for Legend...she knows I'd never hurt her."

Gently, he pinched Colonel Legend's nose. "I can't say how I feel about her in front of you, General. I'm still stuck on how things were on Platirius."

General Revari smiled at him and nodded. "I understand. It'll take some time for all of us to adjust to our new way of life. We'll get through it. Together."

"Will Prince Justin stay here with us?" he asked.

Her eyes clouded. "No. This is no place for him. He's too vulnerable. Now that I've found him again, I don't want to be away from him for a minute, but...I have to protect him. I'll deal with that at the proper time."

While his mother discussed his future with Colonel Legend and Gallium, Prince Justin contemplated his next move. Alone in one of Queen Aiki's enormous bed chambers, he couldn't stop thinking about General Lyric. He gathered that his mother hated her, but something about her grabbed him and made him not want to let go.

He wanted to see her again. He couldn't live on a planet that canceled sex. Maybe he could convince her to leave Platirius?

You're fooling yourself, man. That'll never happen.

He needed to hear her voice. Taking out Colonel Legend's miniature TeleScreen, he studied the controls until he figured out how to operate it. It worked as a transmitter, a phone, and so much more. Could it be voice-activated?

"Only one way to find out." Lifting the small screen to his lips, he said, "General Lyric." Enchanted by the flashes that flew across the screen, he was delighted when her lovely face appeared.

He smiled at her. "Hey, General Lyric."

He expected her to be happy. She wasn't. He tried not to let her wary expression discourage him.

"Prince Justin? This is...a surprise. I didn't expect to see you again. You're still on Kikhani?"

"Yep. I wanted to see how you were doing."

Someone else's face appeared briefly on the screen, a petite woman with dark hair and hazel eyes. She looked from him to General Lyric and smiled before disappearing. General Lyric watched her run off before turning her attention back to him.

"I'm...umm...is something wrong?"

He made himself comfortable on the large bed and crossed his legs. "No, does something have to be wrong for me to want to talk to you?"

Her answer was quick. "Yes."

Dumbfounded, he stared at her. "Are you always so serious?"

She thought for a moment. "Hmm. Yes. It's the only way I know how to be."

Her revelation amazed him. He enjoyed his job but couldn't imagine never stopping to enjoy life. Was life on Platirius really that rigid for her? "Do you ever do anything fun?"

Confused, she cocked her head. "Fun? What's that?"

He peered at her. "Are you messing with me?"

She scrunched up her face. "I don't know what 'messing' means."

"Are you joking about not knowing what fun is?"

Her low, hushed tone soothed him. "I'm telling the truth. There's no need to lie to you."

"Well, first of all, there's no need for us to be so formal. And second..." He scratched at the stubble on his chin. He hadn't had a chance to use the blade his mother had given him. "Fun is what you do outside of work. You know—things you enjoy doing."

She'd rather die than admit it, but she thought the burgeoning beard complemented his appearance. "Well...I enjoy being the leader of the Vivacians."

He frowned. "That's work, Lyric."

She stared into his green eyes. "Work is fun to me. It makes me happy. Does that answer your question?"

It was hard to believe anyone enjoyed fighting people all the time. He wanted to introduce her to experiences she'd never had.

"And yes, being formal is necessary. You're the son of General Revari, and I'm a commoner. On top of that, you're a MaleForm. We don't befriend MaleForms—we're forbidden from personal interactions with them."

"No, Baby. I'm a regular guy. And you're far from common." He sighed in frustration. "It's because of that crazy law Queen Vivant passed."

She carefully assessed him. "I'm not a baby. I'm a full-grown WomanForm."

His eyes caressed her svelte body. "Oh, I can see that."

She ignored the heat rising within her. "Your MotherForm passed it too. Despite what you may think, it's not a stupid law. It protected WomenForms from being hurt by MaleForms. It was the blessing we needed."

He stretched out a hand. "Okay, that's on Platirius. What about everywhere else? Are we trash on other planets too, Lyric?"

She shook her head. "I wouldn't know. I've never lived anywhere except home."

He watched an angry Kikhanian stick her finger in Captain Angela's face. She quickly slapped it away and struck her in the throat. When the Kikhanian reached for her hair, the fight was on. It took a half a dozen Revaltians to pry their captain off the badly beaten soldier.

"Whoa!" he exclaimed.

"What happened?" General Lyric asked. "Are you okay?"

"Yeah, I'm fine. I just watched this fiery little lady—er, I mean, Revaltian beat the hell out of a Kikhanian. I think her name is Captain Angela."

General Lyric's eyes narrowed. "I know exactly who she is. She's several inches shorter than I am, but she almost took my head off with her sword once. She's ruthless, but she earned my respect as a warrior."

Picturing her rolling around on the ground with Captain Angela made him smile, but he kept it to himself. She already had a low opinion of men—he didn't want to give her another reason to ignore him. "I wouldn't want to meet her in a dark alley."

"In a what? What's an alley?"

"Never mind. Hey, why don't you come here and talk to me?"

She raised a single brow. "You want me to come to Kikhani?"

He shrugged. "Sure, why not? I get you and my mother don't like each other—"

Three pairs of eyes peered at her from around a podium. She turned to Captain Kourtney, Sergeant Thea, and Sergeant Alicia.

"There's nothing inappropriate going on," she told them. "We're just talking."

The three Vivacians looked at each other and giggled. She rolled her eyes to the Heavens. She needed to discourage him before the gossip started.

"That's putting it mildly. Your MotherForm hates me. I mean sheer hate. I don't want to have any more trouble with General Revari unless I have to."

"She may not like you, but she loves me. She'd want to see me happy. Talking to you makes me very happy, Lyric."

"How is that? You don't even know who I am."

He leaned back against the headboard. "Well, let's see, you're brave and an amazing fighter. You're the general of an army. You care about your planet and its people. I'd say that makes you a wonderful person."

His compliment warmed her. "Thank you, but I'm not a *person*, I'm a Platirian."

He sighed and rolled his eyes to the ceiling. "Ah, don't get so technical. You know what I mean."

"No, I don't know what you mean. Person means Human. I am not a Human. And, oh—I'm babbling!"

He laughed as she smacked her forehead. "You're cute when you're flustered."

She raised an eyebrow. "Cute? What does that mean?"

"He called her cute," whispered Captain Kourtney.

"What does that mean?" asked Sergeant Alicia.

"Shh, listen! He's gonna tell her what it means," said Sergeant Thea.

"Hmm...it means adorable. Precious. Something that makes me feel warm inside."

"Oooh," said Captain Kourtney. She, Sergeant Thea, and Sergeant Alicia covered their mouths and laughed. They thoroughly enjoyed his bantering with her.

He was right. She was much too serious. It was time for her to have fun. But not on Platirius. Queen Vivant still didn't allow social interactions with MaleForms.

Her insides felt like mush. He was making her feel things she knew she shouldn't. And yet, she couldn't help being drawn to him. "You shouldn't say such things, nor should I listen. All the MaleForms I've known were evil and oppressive. Nothing good will come of this and we should stop now."

"Who puts these crazy ideas in your head? Your precious Queen Vivant? If MaleForms are so evil, then why did she marry one and have his kids? Do you hear how hypocritical that sounds?"

"Things were different for Queen Vivant when General Kron was alive, but not for the rest of us. We've never been treated with respect by MaleForms. For millions of years, they've treated us as less than excrement. What you call a 'crazy' idea has been a lifesaver for me."

Hearing pain in her voice, he sat upright.

"Do you know how it feels to have a MaleForm of a higher rank touch you inappropriately and there's nothing you can do about it? I do."

The TeleScreen trembled slightly in her hand. "Before Platirius split, I almost had my virginity taken from me by MaleForms that were supposed to serve the throne by my side! I'm glad we're never going back to the way things were."

A surge of rage ebbed within him. The thought of anyone hurting her made him want to kill them. "I'm so sorry that happened to you, Lyric. Had I been around, I would've dealt with them. You must know not all men—er, MaleForms are the same, right?"

She shook her head. "I honestly wouldn't know. I've fought with MaleForms, but I've never made friends with any of them. I don't think I'd know how."

His heart skipped a beat. "Then let me show you how it's done. Lyric, we don't have to be enemies. I like you, and I think you're curious about me too. We can build on that."

Her eyes turned cold. "I'm not going to die like Aja," she said firmly.

He blinked. "Who is Aja?"

"She was a soldier who got involved with Simonius. She broke the rules and copulated with him. He killed her before Queen Vivant punished her."

He sat up straighter. He'd seen Simonius get shipped away, but he hadn't known that he'd killed someone. "I see. Well, from what I heard, Simonius was as cold as they come. I'm sorry she lost her life, but that doesn't have anything to do with me. Or you. I have no intentions to harm you. I just want to get to know you."

"You mean you wish to lie with me?"

He opened and closed his mouth as a vision of her nude body shimmered across his mind.

Get it together, Justin.

"That's not the first thing on my mind—no."

He looked her in the eye. "I need you to understand something. When I've taken a woman to my bed, she went willingly. I'm not about forcing myself on a woman—be it friendship or more than that. We can go at your pace. All I'm asking for is a chance."

She was surprised she didn't like imagining him with someone else. She grimaced as an image of General Revari flashed into her mind. "A chance for what? To have me killed? Do you realize who your mother is? She's a very efficient killer. And, again, she hates me. She always has."

"Hm. Noted, but what about you? Do you hate her?"

She didn't hesitate. "I don't like her ways, but I don't hate her. I'm also not crazy enough to cross her."

"So, you don't want to explore what could be because of my mother?"

"Due to a lot of things. I'm in no position to...learn about a MaleForm. I'm not even sure I want to."

She looked up sharply. "I'm being dispatched. I have to go now."

"Duty calls. It's okay, Lyric. I understand. We'll talk again soon."

He noticed her eyes were a lovely shade of purple mixed with gray. She captivated him in ways no other woman had.

"Good-goodnight, Prince Justin," stammered General Lyric.

His voice was as soft as a caress. "Good night, General Lyric."

She disconnected the contact and heard Sergeant Alicia say, "I'm so in loooovvvveeee!" followed by a round of teasing and laughter. "General Lyric has intercepted the ball and scored! Touchdowwwwnnnnn Commoners!" Her teammates doubled over with laughter.

She hid her smile. "You're so off the mark," she said.

A few of the Vivacians started shaking their hips and dancing. Sergeant Alicia missed a step and fell off the bed, still laughing.

"Keep it up and you'll need to visit the medical chamber," said General Lyric.

Their good-natured teasing followed her out the door. The Vivacians adored her. She was firm, yet fair and was the first to offer encouragement in tough times. They were truly happy to hear she and Prince Justin might have a future together.

On the other hand, General Revari was not.

"Shall I kill her?"

Startled, he turned and saw his mother standing in the doorway.

"How—how long have you been standing there?"

She sat down next to him. "Long enough to know you've taken a liking to General Lyric." She was silent for a moment. "You may not realize it now, but Platirian WomenForms despise MaleForms."

"But you fell in love with my dad. You married him and had me. How can you hate men?"

She took the TeleScreen out of his hand. General Lyric was lucky she had disconnected the call before she reached the top of the stairs. "Your father was different. He was a Human and I fell in love with him while I was away from Platirius. Had it been the other way around and he traveled to Platirius instead of me going to Earth, we never would've been together."

Her grip on the small TeleScreen tightened. "Millions of years of oppression and bitterness created a wide gulf between some WomenForms and MaleForms. I say 'some' because there are cases where there's been love matches."

She shook her head at memories of General Kron being iron-hard on the battlefield, yet nearly tripping over himself to please her vain, vile sister when he wasn't fighting. "But the majority of the SexForms reviled each other long before Queen Vivant and I decreed to get rid of MaleForms."

His heart was heavy. He wasn't sure if he wanted to know, but he had to ask. "How did you get rid of them?"

"We packed them up into death crafts and sent them into the sun with King Dubian. We felt compelled to make such a drastic change. I didn't want WomenForms to continue living in fear of MaleForms."

Her clear, low voice easily carried over the noise outside the window. "I grew tired of them believing they were better than us and lording their physical strength over us. I despise General Lyric, but I agree with much of what she said."

She pushed her tiny frame back to rest against the headboard. He wondered how a woman so small could kill so many men.

"There are not many WomenForms who haven't been touched against their will or called nasty names. She was lucky it didn't go any further. MaleForms fully believed they had the right to violate and beat WomenForms whenever they wanted."

She craned her neck to look up at him. He outweighed her by over a hundred pounds and towered above her, yet she'd never see him as anything more than her baby.

"King Dubian and King Anemi cultivated an environment that was dangerous and toxic for WomenForms. They never lifted a hand to shield them. Queen Vivant and I were spared from that because we were royal WomenForms, but commoners had no such protection."

She crossed her tiny leg onto his large, muscular one. "I'd never agree to you being with Lyric anyway, or any WomanForm for that matter. If you're going to fall in love, do it with a Human woman. At least she'd understand you better."

He shook his head. "Now you're telling me who to love? Do you think that's fair?"

"Are you going to give up on all Human women due to one emotionally unavailable WomanForm?"

"You did. You never loved anyone except my dad."

"Because there's no one in the galaxy or on Earth who will ever fill your father's place in my heart. The years I spent with him will last for the rest of my lifespan. I can't imagine being with anyone else. I want you to know how that kind of love feels, but forget about Lyric."

Her nose wrinkled in distaste. "She'd be an idiot even if she wasn't a Platirian. She's not good enough for you."

His laugh sounded like Oliver's. It was music to her ears. "No, she's not good enough for you, but I think she's perfect." He laughed again when she made a face. "It sounds like you've never let Dad go."

She smiled. "Never. Now that I've found you, I'm never letting you go either. I want to know every detail of your life. We're never going to be apart again." She hugged him fiercely until he grimaced.

"Uh...Mom?"

"Hmmm?"

"You're stronger than most men I know. You're breaking my ribs."

Immediately, she broke the embrace. "Oh! Sorry!"

They smiled at each other.

"Get some rest. Tomorrow, Queen Aiki and I leave for Earth. I'll leave you here under Colonel Legend's protection. Once my business with her is finished, you're going back to Earth."

"You're not letting me stay here with you? You just said we weren't going to be apart."

She reached for his hand. "We won't be. Do you realize I can teleport myself anywhere in seconds? You have to return to your life on Earth. You are a hybrid MaleForm who is unskilled for battle. You can't defend yourself against the kings of the galaxy."

"You can teach me how to fight!"

She moved her leg away from his. "That's not going to happen."

"Why not? Are you scared I'll die?"

"Precisely. I'm not going to gamble with your life. I lost your father. I won't lose you too."

He glared at her. "Mom, I'm not a baby!"

"There will be no argument about this. You're safer on Earth."

"The Apocalypse is going on. Did you forget that?"

"I forget nothing. I'll be there to shield you from it."

"I don't need my mommy to protect me! I'm a grown man! Don't treat me like a child!"

She leapt off the bed with the agility of a cat. "You will do what I tell you to do!" she thundered.

"Are all the women here crazy, or is it just you? My mother never spoke to me that way," he muttered.

He shivered as a chill entered the room. Images of what she'd done to the traitorous Revaltians came flooding back to him.

"She may have reared you, but that woman isn't your mother." He observed the quick shift in her mood.

She looks like an evil character in a video game.

"Why do your eyes look like laser beams? We've just met, and now you're powering up to kill me?"

"Don't be foolish," she snapped. "Never mention that Human woman to me again. I was robbed of being your MotherForm. Until recently, I didn't know you were alive."

Prince Justin sighed. "I know, and I'm sorry. I shouldn't have said that. Wait—that's the second time I heard that. What's a MotherForm?"

"It's our formal word for Mother." Her calm tone belied the rage clouding her face.

Pissing her off isn't a smart move, idiot.

Raising his hands, he said, "I don't want to get off on the wrong foot with you, General. I'm not a fighter."

She wiped away a tear. "Neither was Oliver. He never got angry with me. He was my peace."

Her sadness tore at his heart. "Oh, Mama." He stood, pulling her into a strong embrace. "Listen, the last thing I want to do is hurt you. I came because I wanted to finally know who you are. I know it's hard, but you have to see me as a grown man and allow me to make my own choices."

Stepping back to look down at her, he wiped her tears and said, "I realize what happened to you and my father was unfair, but I'm not a child. I don't need protecting."

She nodded firmly. "Yes, you do. Outside of Earth, it's a new game. I'm determined to protect you—even if it costs me my life. No one will stop me from keeping you safe. Not even you."

He dropped his head when she turned and left him alone. His mother treated him like a baby and the woman he was slowly falling in love with was afraid to return his feelings. He sighed. Space was definitely beginning to seem like a reality TV show.

Chapter 7

Queen Aiki looked up from watching Humans on her TranScreen to Prince Justin standing in her doorway. She ogled his tall, muscular frame and smiled.

"Why, the son of General Revari has come to see me. I'm honored. What may I do for you?"

"My mother says we're leaving for Earth tomorrow. I won't be returning, so I'd like to have a tour of Kikhani. Is that okay?"

"Of course, Prince Justin. It would be my pleasure. What would you like to see first?"

He pointed to a building standing farther away from the others. "What's over there?"

Her smile faltered a bit. "That's my research chamber. Why? Do you want to go there?"

"Ah. So, it's a research chamber. I suspected it was a medical facility or something. I'm a doctor, so naturally, it interests me."

"Um," she said, struggling to find a reason not to let him see it. To her credit, she wasn't a very good liar. She finally gave up looking for a rational excuse. "All right, let us go so you can have a look."

He hid a smile. While dining with Gallium and Dr. Barrios, he'd noticed something strange: a Kikhanian soldier—the same one he'd killed in battle—leaving the research chamber. Under the power of King Dubian's BrainStaff, it wasn't possible she had survived a broken neck.

So how was she now walking around as if nothing had happened? Her mannerisms were strange too. She didn't laugh or speak. To Prince Justin, she was an empty shell.

A clone? Did Queen Aiki have the ability to clone her warriors?

They entered what appeared to be a large laboratory. It was more state-of-the-art than anywhere he'd been back home. She looked up at him. She wasn't ugly, but General Lyric was already in his system.

"Here's where I keep my secrets," she said.

Grabbing her face, he pulled her closer to him, nuzzling against her neck. "I want you to tell me all of your secrets." He traced her earlobe with the tip of his finger. "All of them," he whispered against her ear.

She traced his lips with the tip of her finger. "If I show you, then you'll have to stay and be my king."

"I'll be whatever you need me to be. Hold on," he said, tilting his head to peer down at her. "Do you have any weapons on you?"

"No, not a one. Now, would I hurt a handsome MaleForm like you?"

She melted when he smiled. Like his mother, at times he used his looks to get what he wanted. "Of course you would," he said, rubbing his hand down her spine. "Let's see if you're hiding anything."

She shuddered as he continued rubbing his hand down the base of her spine and up to her long, supple neck. Gently, he cradled it in his hand, kissing her deeply.

Her breasts swelled against his firm chest and she moaned, craving more of his touch. And he gave it to her—a quick zap from General Revari's Brainstaff knocked her out cold.

He'd hit her so quickly, she hadn't realized he was carrying the BrainStaff in his backpack. It gave him just enough strength to overpower her. He tossed aside her limp body as if she weighed no more than a paperclip and sighed. He figured she'd be out for a while.

"Sorry, Queen Aiki, but you're just not my type. I'm more interested in finding out what you do in here."

He looked around at the various machines and tables. Kikhani was a stark contrast to Platirius. It had none of the impressive platinum and chrome buildings. The planet was gold and most of the furnishings were made from solid gold.

However, Queen Aiki's paltry lack of taste cheapened what could've been an exquisite palace. Only her advanced research chamber was impressive. Very. He was disappointed nothing stood out that would solve the mystery of the dead warrior.

He tried to open a door but it was locked. The keycode had a scanner around it. Whatever she was hiding had to be in there! He scooped her up in his arms.

"Up-sa-daisy!" He carried her over to the door and pressed her hand on the scanner.

"Greetings, Queen Aiki," said a female automated voice.

When the door opened, he stepped inside and gently set her on the floor. Grinning ear to ear, he found more than he'd bargained for. Dozens of bodies were held in large capsules of thick, gold liquid.

He perused the faces. They all looked the same. So, Queen Aiki *was* making clones! It made sense. The Kikhanian warriors were skilled fighters, but most of them didn't speak or interact with each other.

Now he understood why. They had only been trained to fight. They also had terrible tempers. If one turned on another, killing her, then a replacement was needed. She had begun cloning her warriors to replenish her army.

But was it the only reason? She had enough equipment to make a thousand clones at a time. He sat at a gigantic computer at the end of the hall. The BrainStaff gave him the ability to read Kikhanian language.

For hours, he sat learning how she ran Kikhani. He uncovered three planets highlighted on the screen. All were marked *Kikhanian territory*. Realizing what she'd done, he mentally connected with General Revari, asking her to come to the research chamber.

She looked down at Queen Aiki lying on the floor. "Prince Justin, what have you done?"

He glanced over at her. "I just knocked her out. She'll be fine. Look, Mom. See these three planets? She's placed clones on all of them. All of the...you call them Beings...she swiped to fuel Kikhani were replaced with clones. The fourth planet is Earth, but she doesn't have enough there to claim it."

He pointed to the screen. "These planets all belong to her, but she never absorbed them into Kikhani. Why?"

"She didn't know how," said General Revari. "First, you have to claim many souls before you can absorb a planet. Second, it takes mental concentration to merge planets together. King Hitam never taught her to do it, so these planets have lain dormant with nothing living on them except her clones."

"When you kill King Hitam and absorb his powers, doesn't that mean you can take the planets by default?"

She smiled. "Yes, you've caught on to all this without my having to teach you. I'm impressed!"

He smiled back at her. "Queen Vivant stole Platirius from you. I want you to have all the power you need to defeat her."

"I'm happy. More than you know. I can't wait to get to Earth and get rid of King Hitam. These planets were once run by three different kings. She must have lain with them and murdered them. Since she didn't absorb the planets into Kikhani, their essence remains within them."

"So after you deal with the Hitam dude, all of their knowledge and power will be transferred to you?"

"Exactly." She looked at him. "Please tell me you didn't copulate with her."

Shaking his head, he shuddered. "I'm buzzed, but not that drunk, Mom. No thanks."

"Thank the Heavens."

"Believe it or not, I do have standards."

"Of course you do. You're my ChildForm."

He laughed and looked at her BrainStaff. He lifted it, examining it closely. "There's some pretty powerful stuff going on with this thing."

She grabbed it from his hands. "Give it to me. I don't want its powers influencing you."

He shrugged. "I've already learned to absorb some of the BrainStaff's power." He looked at her hands. "You know, it's hard to believe those little hands of yours have killed so many people."

Astonished by his confession, she stared at him. There was nothing she could do about him being the grandson of King Dubian. It didn't sit well with her that his spirit had the power to control Prince Justin from the grave.

As much as she wanted to keep him with her on Kikhani, it wasn't possible. The old dead kings—eager to reclaim their power through a male descendant—would never allow him to rest.

"How is that possible?"

He shrugged one shoulder. "I don't know. It talks to me in a language I've never heard. But somehow, I understand it."

"That's because you belong to my bloodline," she said. You have to be careful with our powers. They can control you if you let them."

Oliver had never been irritated with her. If he had, their son's angry countenance would've been the perfect example.

"Will you please stop treating me like a toddler? I'm not interested in power or acquiring planets. I'm doing all of this for you."

She sighed. Was this how MotherForms and ChildForms interacted? He even pouted like her. Shaking her head, she directed her attention to the floating bodies in the tanks.

"You don't seem surprised about the clones," said Prince Justin.

"I'm not," she admitted. "I've done business with Queen Aiki before. That's how she slipped the transmitter on me and brought me here. I think many of the Kikhanians are clones."

She pointed to a button. "This keeps them alive. If this is activated, they'll all fall. I'm sure she never wanted anyone to find out about this. Without an army, it wouldn't take long to defeat her."

They looked at the numerous tanks that filled nearly half of the research chamber. "Are you going to keep them around?"

She twisted her mouth. "For now. I can sacrifice them in a battle without having to use my own soldiers until I build up my army again."

She peered closer at the screen. "She even cloned the soldiers on these planets. She should've recruited them into her army instead of using them for energy."

"What will you do with the clones?" asked Prince Justin.

She traced a large decorative "R" on one of the tanks. "For the moment? Nothing. If I need them, I'll train them to fight. She has thousands in here. Good work, son. I'm going up to plan how to take down Hitam. Are you coming?"

He zoomed in on the screen to carefully examine the planets. "In a minute. I'm going to look at a few more things."

She kissed him on the forehead. "Don't be long."

"Hey, my first forehead kiss," he teased. "Goodnight, General."

He leaned back in his chair, staring up at the rows of strange bodies. "So, you have thousands of clones, huh?" He pivoted in the chair to look at Queen Aiki's sleeping form. "You won't mind if I borrow a few, right?"

If one saw him smiling, they'd swear he resembled King Dubian. He pushed a small button. "Gallium, can you come to the research chamber?"

"Sure. I'll be there in a minute."

"Don't tell anyone you're coming."

Gallium paused. *What is he up to now?*

"All right. I'm coming."

Gallium stood in awe of all the clones she'd made. "So she's been conquering planets, but not using their power?"

"Mama said she doesn't know how."

"Thank the Heavens! If she did, Kikhani would be as powerful as Platirius by now and would be a major force to defeat." Carefully, he inspected everything.

The vast array of machines was of particular interest to him. "I never would've guessed something this impressive would've been on Kikhani. It reminds me of the research chamber we had back home."

"Yeah, Platirius looks like something in the movies."

Gallium looked at him. "I meant Coldarius. I'm not a Platirian."

Prince Justin couldn't hide his surprise. "The planet King Dubian destroyed?" He rubbed his head. "Man, the surprises keep coming. How did you end up on Platirius?"

Gallium continued inspecting the clones. "It's ancient history," he said quietly.

Prince Justin felt he didn't want to talk about his past, so he changed the subject. "Gallium, what did Queen Vivant's daughters look like?"

He looked at him sharply. "Why do you want to know that?"

Prince Justin turned to look at him. Staring into his eyes, Gallium felt a wave of uneasiness. The more time he spent outside of Earth, the more he became like King Dubian and King Anemi.

"Do you have photos of them?"

Gallium tugged on his beard. "No, but I can pull their profiles up in this system." He punched in a few numbers. "Here they are. That's Princesses Teenah, Tyre, and Tarah."

Prince Justin looked at the princesses and laughed. "They're triplets! That makes it even easier."

Gallium cocked his head. "It makes what easier, Prince Justin?"

Prince Justin met his eyes again. "It seems General Lyric is very fond of Queen Vivant. I'm not...and you're not. So why not have a little fun with Queen Iceburg?"

Gallium considered that. "What do you have in mind?"

"Have you ever heard of Halloween?" asked Prince Justin, looking up at the clones.

Gallium blinked, shaking his head. "No, I haven't."

"It's a holiday Humans celebrate and say 'trick or treat.' You and I are going to play a trick on Queen Vivant she'll never forget."

After supper, Queen Vivant and General Lyric strolled around one of the spectacular royal gardens. Queen Vivant decided that whatever was going on between General Revari and Queen Aiki was their business.

As long as it didn't involve Platirius or Earth, she needn't trouble herself. However, if she learned they planned to usurp either realm, Platirius would be ready.

General Lyric had her own dilemma to ponder. She didn't understand why Prince Justin had contacted her. She thought there were hundreds of WomenForms that were far more beautiful than she. She didn't have a feminine bone in her body. There was no reason for him to take an interest in her.

Although she tried to be logical about the situation, unfamiliar feelings fluttered within her. She didn't want to admit it, but she found herself thinking about him more than she should. She'd been surprised he'd asked her to come to Kikhani. Even more surprising, for a split second, she had contemplated acquiescing to his request.

There was no reason to see him. Was this how Aja had felt about Simonius? She hoped not. She'd worked too hard on her career to end up like Aja—her life and career now a distant memory.

"I just don't understand why he called," she said for the third time. "I've never given him the slightest reason to think we'd connect on any level."

Queen Vivant picked a flower and handed it to her. "Sometimes things sneak up on us out of the blue. How do you feel about him asking to meet with you? Do you think his request was genuine?"

She recalled her talk with him. "Well...yes. It didn't seem as if he was setting me up for an ambush. I think he wanted to see me alone. But...I'm not free with my body. He understood that the first time we met. It was a waste of his time to contact me. And mine."

"Let's sit by the lilies," suggested Queen Vivant. "You feel it was a waste of time...but he didn't. He offered you friendship, but I'd say he's rather smitten with you."

General Lyric's mouth dropped. Speechless, she stared at her mentor, at a loss at how to respond. "But he doesn't have a reason to be interested in me."

"So you think. But what you think has nothing to do with how he may feel."

She shook her head. "I don't understand. He knows I'm a Platirian and he's a hybrid. He has no clue about how to survive here. Second, he's...well, he's King Dubian's grandson. The BrainStaff made him so...disrespectful. The things he said were disgusting."

"Mm. And how did he sound without the BrainStaff?"

She thought about that for a moment. "He was kind. Thoughtful. He gave me a lot of compliments. I can tell when one doesn't mean what they say, but I didn't feel he tried to appeal to my ego." She sighed. " I think he generally likes me."

Queen Vivant observed her closely. General Lyric kept her hair cut short to avoid styling it. She wasn't interested in keeping up with the fashionable hairstyles most Platirian WomenForms wore.

Except for a single silver necklace—gifted to her by her mother—she never wore jewelry. Or makeup. Queen Vivant wondered if she'd agree to a makeover. If she did, it would fit beautifully into her new plans for Platirius.

"I was honest with him when I said we shouldn't be friends. That's the way it should be. I love Platirius and my community. There's no way I'd leave it for a MaleForm. I think falling in love is dumb."

Queen Vivant laughed. "Oh? You do?"

She gave her a sheepish look. "Present company excluded, my queen. I meant falling in love would be dumb for me. If others wanted to...then the consequences would be on them."

Queen Vivant flashed a carbon copy of her mother's smile. "Oh, I don't know, Lyric. Sometimes love is a good thing. So good for us it makes us better at who we are and what we do. There's a lot a WomanForm may accomplish on her own, but two working together toward the same goals is always better than being alone."

She watched two rabbits running across a field. "You've stated why you shouldn't be friends, but emotions aren't often dictated by sound logic. You say you were honest with him. Have you extended the same level of honesty to yourself? Can you admit he's never moved you to feel anything at all?"

General Lyric stared down at her feet. She wasn't ready to explore any burgeoning feelings toward Prince Justin.

Queen Vivant gave her a soft poke in the ribs. "Are you blushing, General?"

"Queen Vivant." Her groan was drowned out by the sound of the queen's peal of laughter.

"Well? I'm waiting."

"The first night we met...and when we spoke again...I felt...I don't know how to describe it. Little flutters in my stomach. When I hear his voice, I catch myself wanting to keep him talking. It's crazy! I don't know him."

General Lyric expelled a frustrated breath. "And he's General Revari's son. He might have her temper and mean-spiritedness, for all I know. I can't give any MaleForm that kind of power over me. I won't end up like Aja!"

"But you're not Aja, so get that out of your mind. Your situation with Prince Justin has nothing to do with what happened to her. You're using her as an excuse not to confront what's happening to you."

"What *is* happening?"

Queen Vivant's eyes sparkled with mischief. "It's love, Lyric. Love isn't something you can explain away or reason with. It comes when you least expect it. When it does...sometimes you're powerless to do anything except bask in it."

"Is that how you felt about General Kron?"

She picked a lily and carefully began removing its soft, sweet petals. "Oooh, yes. At my father's LifeCelebration, I saw this big, broad-shouldered MaleForm walking toward me and almost died. His eyes were silver like mine, but they sparkled. His lashes were much longer than mine too. The first time he spoke to me, I nearly melted. I could barely speak."

"By The One. That sounds awful."

She turned to face her. "Why awful, Lyric?"

"Because it means he had power over you."

"Oh? He had the power to do what? Turn me into a witless fool?" She shook her head softly. "No. Love may be powerful, but when you're loved by the right one, nothing about it is wrong."

Her voice broke as she struggled to keep her emotions in check. "When he didn't return from the last battle, I wanted to curl up and die. I didn't want to leave my bed, but I had to. I had three little ones who depended on me. Losing him was hard, but I had to go on...for them."

"It was a love match between you and General Kron. That's no life for me. You freed us when you sent all the MaleForms into the sun. Now, we no longer have to worry about being assaulted and oppressed."

"I've often wondered if Queen Revari and I made the right decision. Platirius was corrupted by evil so deep it spread to the very roots beneath our feet. There was too much tension and hatred between the SexForms."

Queen Vivant stopped fiddling with the lily. "We didn't want the cycle of exploitation to continue. Our goal was to give our WomenForms a fresh start."

The doubt in her tone surprised General Lyric. "And you've done it. We have nothing to fear anymore."

"Yes, but at what cost? Here you are, suspicious of Prince Justin's motives, when it could be all he wants is to be good to you—nothing more. I never meant for you to continue being wary of MaleForms. I see now we solved only half of the issue."

Queen Vivant shook her head sadly. "I'm able to see both sides, for I know how true love feels. Yet, how many WomenForms feel as you do? Afraid to love and to trust your hearts? This isn't the outcome I intended. Not all MaleForms are terrible."

"With all due respect, My Queen, you sound like Prince Justin."

She smiled. "At times, family members think alike. Your experiences with the opposite SexForm have shaped your perception. The same could be said for him. I'm not saying you're wrong for feeling the way you do."

She looked up at a life-sized statue of her father she couldn't bring herself to tear down. "Prince Justin is a descendant of my father. You are right to be wary of him. Father's BrainStaff changed his personality in seconds."

Instinctively, General Lyric shivered. The evil power of the BrainStaff had made her fear him.

"I have no doubt if he were to remain on Platirius, it would be a continuation of the legacy I tried to erase. But he's from Earth. He grew up in a completely different environment. Maybe if you gave into your feelings, you and he could have a fresh start away from Platirius."

"Queen Vivant!" exclaimed General Lyric. "I don't want to leave Platirius for Prince Justin!"

"And I don't want to lose the best general my army has ever had, but I don't want to hold you back, Lyric. Now, if you genuinely have no feelings for my nephew—"

"I don't have feelings for him!"

Queen Vivant looked as if she didn't believe her, but she said, "Then it's settled. I won't pry into your personal life anymore."

General Lyric shook her head firmly. "I don't have a personal life. Everything I love is right here on Platirius. I'm devoted to my job. I don't want anything to change."

"I understand and respect your wishes. I simply don't want you to feel love is wrong when it isn't. General Revari doesn't know this, but I spied on her for quite a long time before I told our father where she was."

Although seeing Queen Dellah again had comforted her, she still hadn't rid herself of her guilt for tearing apart her sister's family. "Prince Justin's father was a very kind Being. I couldn't admit it then, but he was good to her."

The queen stared glumly at her feet. "He made her happier than I ever could, and for that, I was jealous. I wanted her to be happy here—not with strangers. It was my hatred and prejudice against the Humans that tore her family apart. After she lost them...she changed. Her contempt for Humans began to rival my own. She still blames his parents for turning them in."

She stared off into the distance. "Hoping she'd forget about them, I withheld the truth from her."

Chapter 8

Her gaze shifted to the king's statue again. "His sister betrayed her, but his parents refused to bend to Father's will. He made an example of them because…they loved her. Their love for her made him even more insane."

She remembered the instructions given to her by Queen Dellah in her dream. She had to find a way to get through to General Revari.

"To them, she was their daughter. They refused to betray her. I never told her because a part of me was angry that she loved a Human family more than her own. I was wrong to interfere with her happiness. I'm still paying for that mistake, Lyric."

General Lyric took her hand. She was only a few years younger than her leader. Losing both parents at a young age had made her an orphan. Her foster parents had told her that her mother died under mysterious circumstances shortly after relocating from Coldarius to Platirius, and her father had been killed on a rescue mission.

That was all she knew about her past. She grew up as a commoner and eventually ascended the ranks within Platirius's army. She looked up to her as her queen and as a sister.

General Revari might've disagreed, but Queen Vivant had given her the love and support she needed to grow into the fierce and spirited young Being she was. Proud to lead Platirius's army—she was willing to walk through fire if her queen asked her to.

She didn't feel she was losing out on anything—especially love. Her purpose was to protect Platirius until the end of her lifespan. She had an amazing leader, plenty of friends, and a warm and loving community. Nor did she need a MaleForm to be happy. Her life was complete as it was. She hoped Prince Justin would find that level of contentment one day.

"I'm not used to speaking with MaleForms about anything other than strategizing and fighting. It felt strange."

"It feels that way at first," said Queen Vivant. "But pretty soon, one conversation develops into more. Much more. I'll never tell you to compromise who you are, but at times, things catch us off guard."

She wagged her finger at the general. "Not that I'm telling you to pursue anything with him. You're already on my sister's bad side. You don't need any more grief from her regarding her son."

General Lyric grimaced. "Agreed. I do wish him all the best."

"So do I. We didn't get off to a great start, but I wish him no harm. You've added a new goal for me to bring to fruition. Although many WomenForms still eschew the idea of forming meaningful partnerships with MaleForms, many do not."

Her determined look piqued General Lyric's curiosity. "It would be better to allow love to be nurtured and grow than to face punishment for copulation. I feel very ashamed and guilty for what happened to Aja."

"That wasn't your fault. Aja knew the rules. She chose to break them. You can't hold yourself responsible for everything that happens."

"No, her demise is definitely my fault. Had I been a better commander, she might have been saved. Simonius was such a terrible choice for her. I must take responsibility for all that happens or I'd be a poor excuse for a leader."

Queen Vivant looked at two birds splashing in a birdbath. "I don't regret purging MaleForms from Platirius. The evil that permeated our borders was woven too deeply into their minds."

She smiled at General Lyric. "Now? I have a new idea. I'd like to expand our borders to allow MaleForms from other planets to live on Platirius. Without the Platirian curse, WomenForms would be free to love again without fear of being exploited."

The queen tapped her foot, thinking hard. "Of course, they would need to be heavily scrutinized before obtaining citizenship. I want to continue moving us forward."

"Do you think you'll ever be open to love again?"

Queen Vivant shook her head. "I don't think so. I doubt I'll find anyone who could make me feel the way Lucian did."

She looked up toward the sky. "Yet, what happens in our futures is determined by The One. I'm fully open to His will. Let's go back inside. We need to lay out the new menus for the dining staff."

General Lyric surveyed the beautiful gardens and smiled. "Yes, My Queen."

As she exited, she wondered if he was thinking about her. She also wondered why she cared. Queen Vivant thought love caught you by surprise, but she hoped it would pass over her and knock someone else off their feet. She had no time for love.

Queen Vivant had called for all Platirians to meet outside the gates of the palace to declare a new proclamation. One she hoped would change Platirius for the better.

"I completely understand if some of you wish not to engage with MaleForms," she said. "After what happened to Aja, I'm not surprised you'd be wary. I don't regret ordering the Mass Deaths with my sister. The perilous magic of these grounds had corrupted their minds against us. Platirius could not continue going in such a toxic direction."

She scanned the faces in the crowd. "What I want to make clear is that evil magic only affected *some* of the MaleForms when my ancestors ruled Platirius. My late husband, General Kron, hailed from Maieman. Gallium and Dr. Barrios came from Coldarius before it was destroyed."

Recognition glowed in the faces of some of the older WomenForms. The presence of the Coldarians was still strong on Platirius.

"Even the transplant soldiers who took advantage of King Dubian's tyranny corrupted themselves. There was no saving them. Now, Platirius is free from all the misogyny that plagued us."

She watched the WomenForms look around at each other. Needing to know how they felt, she quickly scanned their minds. While many were open to the possibility of extending grace to MaleForms outside of Platirius, some of them shared General Lyric's views and rejected her offer to open Platirius's borders to allow MaleForms to live among them.

Still, her new proposal had more supporters than detractors. That gave her hope.

"I and members of the justice council will carefully vet every MaleForm who applies to live on Platirius. Only the best will be chosen. No criminals or WomenForm haters will be allowed to live here."

Every eye was on Queen Vivant. A few murmurs of curiosity rose within the crowd. She was pleased to see some were intrigued by her new plan.

"You have my word, your safety will remain my top priority. We'll begin open interviews next week. If you don't wish to form relationships with a MaleForm, that is your right. General Lyric? Please share with us what you and Captain Kourtney have been working on."

General Lyric bowed to Queen Vivant and took her place at the podium. "We've designed a new task force that will specifically address any crimes committed against WomenForms.

If any MaleForm is found guilty, he will be executed in the Flames of Justice. Immediately."

General Lyric's fiery words captured the essence of the new reform Queen Vivant envisioned for Platirius. "That will send a strong message to every MaleForm outside of our borders that we won't tolerate any sign of aggression toward WomenForms."

All of the WomenForms raised their fists in agreement.

"We want all of you to feel safe and we intend to ensure it happens. Please direct all questions to me and Captain Kourtney. Thank you."

She stepped away so Queen Vivant could continue with the meeting. The WomenForms admired the determination in their ruler's tone.

"If necessary, I'll make arrangements for you to meet with me to address any concerns you may have. Also, my decree of never allowing a MaleForm to rule Platirius still stands. It will never be abolished. Platirius has prospered under the direction of WomenForms. We will continue with the new order."

She smiled at the loud round of applause and cheers that erupted from the WomenForms. "I'm glad that makes you happy. If there's nothing else, I'll let you return to your duties. Thank you for all you do to support Platirius."

O n Kikhani, Prince Justin was indeed thinking of General Lyric. The mysterious powers he absorbed from General Revari's BrainStaff allowed him to scan her mind, giving him inconspicuous insight into her thoughts.

"There's so much more to life than being her sidekick, Lyric."

He shaved the last of his beard and brought a warm, moist towel to his face. Staring at his reflection, he vowed to get Queen Vivant out of his way.

T he next morning, he met Gallium in the research chamber. "I'm processing the last batch of Callidut. General Revari wants to use it as a weapon. I'm willing to lend you a few bottles, but as for the rest of your plan, I can't be a part of that."

The strange colors flowing in Gallium's eyes made him pause.

"General Revari is a traditional WomanForm. She's against MaleForms attacking WomenForms. You're her son, so she won't hold anything against you. But I've been given the chance to make a new start here. I don't intend to make the same mistake Simonius did."

Prince Justin nodded, taking the bottles from him. "Understood. Thanks to my new powers, I teleported to Platirius undetected and got what I needed. So, you and my aunt Legend are going to make a go of it, huh?"

Gallium blushed. "Uh…"

Prince Justin burst out laughing. "This is too funny. All the Aliens are scared to admit they have feelings. You should visit Earth. I'll take you to a few strip clubs to loosen you up."

Gallium set the Callidut on the table. "I've been to some. I was walking around Earth before you were even thought of, Prince Justin."

Prince Justin raised an eyebrow. He was beginning to like Gallium even more.

Gallium counted the remaining bottles of Callidut. There was more than enough left for General Revari. "If she becomes addicted, taking Platirius will be a cakewalk. You should know that once everyone finds out Queen Vivant is acting loopy again, Platirius will get attacked from all sides."

Prince Justin opened a bottle to sniff its contents, but Gallium stopped him. "You don't want to inhale it. It won't kill you, but it will alter your mind on a dangerous level. And be very careful not to get it on your skin."

Grateful for Gallium's warning, he quickly re-corked the bottle.

"When Queen Vivant was going out of her mind, Platirius was safe—no one wanted to step on General Revari's toes. If you succeed in getting her to take the Callidut again, you'll be placing your mother in a delicate situation too."

Gallium took the bottle from him, checking to make sure he'd sealed it properly before returning it. "The other kings don't know she's on Kikhani, but they know she's not on Platirius to protect it anymore. General Kron taught his wife how to fight, so she can hold her own. Still, it's General Revari whom they fear the most."

He looked steadily at Prince Justin. "They won't just attack Queen Vivant. They'll also come for you. Both of King Anemi's sons are dead. The other kings won't risk the chance of a MaleForm descendant becoming the leader of Platirius again. It won't matter that General Revari is your mother. They'll go around her to get to you."

Gallium began organizing the bottles of Callidut. "She's the best warrior in the galaxy. Yet, if the other kings come together as a united force...things could go badly for her too, not just Queen Vivant."

Prince Justin watched silently, fascinated by the speed of Gallium's hands. "If I were you, I'd play around with the Callidut—just don't draw it out. King Hitam isn't as healthy as he used to be. It won't take long before she kills him. If a war breaks out, you'll want her to be close."

Gallium looked over at Queen Aiki, still asleep on the floor. "Don't expect her to be any help. She's relied on these...things to help her win wars. If this place is bombed, there goes half of her army."

"I'll be careful," said Prince Justin. "Right now, my focus is on bringing her down a notch or two."

Gallium nodded. "I wish you luck. It serves her right."

"Why is General Lyric so close to her? Doesn't she have a family of her own?"

When Gallium went silent, he wondered if he'd struck a nerve. Finally, he said, "General Lyric is a Coldarian, like me and Colonel Legend."

Prince Justin couldn't hide his surprise. "I never would've guessed she came from there too. What happened to her family?"

"King Dubian killed them. Her father died flying over Coldarius. After Coldarius was absorbed, there wasn't enough energy to sustain it. General Lyric's parents were General Iham and Lady Alarah."

Gallium frowned. "I didn't like Lady Alarah's arrogant ways, but General Iham was a good MaleForm and an excellent leader in Coldarius's army."

Quickly finishing with one batch of Callidut, he started on another. "General Lyric takes after her father. It's in her blood to lead. I don't like giving her credit, but she's good at what she does. I wasn't surprised when Queen Vivant appointed her general to her army."

That explains why she's so serious, thought Prince Justin. "Did her mother die in the freeze too?"

Gallium's fist clenched. "No, she died long before that. I won't go into detail, but let's just say she got what she deserved. I don't like General Lyric, but I'll never tell her about her mother. It would destroy her."

Admiring his sense of integrity, he realized Gallium was an honorable MaleForm. "What about her father? Did he fight Queen Vivant's husband to save Coldarius?"

"General Iham? No. King Dubian got rid of him before he could help anyone," said Gallium. "King Dubian deceived everyone—including Queen Opal—into believing Coldarius would continue merging peacefully with Platirius. King Carlomon had no idea how treacherous King Dubian was. None of us did, until it was too late."

Now finished with packaging the Callidut, he set it aside. "I have to let it rest before I contain it. Otherwise, it'll explode under pressure. By that time, he'd transported everyone he needed to expand his empire."

Fury clouded his handsome face. "If it weren't for Queen Dellah, I would've been left behind too. She brought me to Platirius before she married King Dubian."

Confused, Prince Justin asked, "I thought Queen Dellah was my grandmother. Who is Queen Opal?"

"Queen Opal and Queen Dellah were twin sisters. King Dubian married her after Queen Dellah died giving birth to General Revari."

Gallium grimaced. "King Dubian was a sick MaleForm. His obsession with Queen Dellah made most of us uncomfortable—even her."

He placed the Callidut inside a safe box only he could access. "Queen Dellah realized she'd made a mistake by marrying him. By then, she was already carrying General Revari. She tried her best to shield everyone from his craziness."

Prince Justin wished he could've met Queen Dellah. "No one missed him when he died, did they?"

Gallium's laugh was filled with bitterness. "Not a soul. Queen Vivant ordered the flags to be lowered on Platineous, but I think she did it out of duty. General Revari threw a lavish party on Rubarius. We celebrated well into the next morning."

Prince Justin scanned the lock on the box. He could crack the code if he wanted to, but earning Gallium's respect was important to him. If he ran out, he'd just ask for more. "My mother, the killer, likes to party?"

For the first time since talking about Coldarius, Gallium smiled. "There are a lot of things about her you don't know. She can be a lot of fun when she wants to be. As for Queen Opal, she believed he'd make Coldarius even more prosperous, but in the end, he betrayed her and King Carlomon."

Sensing Gallium was ready to talk about the most painful part of his past, Prince Justin sat down beside him.

"Soon, gossip started going around. It didn't take long before it reached Queen Opal. Rumor had it she was organizing a revolt against King Dubian. She wanted him dead for what he did to Coldarius. Then, one night, she was found dead. Her throat was slashed."

Prince Justin was intrigued. "Who killed her?"

Gallium shrugged. "No one knows. The murder weapon was found on one of the guards, but I never believed he was the killer. He wasn't smart enough to carry out a royal's murder. After Queen Opal's death, King Dubian covered everything up. No one ever mentioned her or Coldarius again. They were too afraid of King Dubian."

"Wow... Platirius was filled with drama back in the day," said Prince Justin.

Gallium nodded solemnly. "It still is. Even though the Ice Queen would like to believe she alone has the power to change Platirius, there are still more than a few Platirians who remember things as they were. The ghosts of the past still walk among the grounds. They aren't going anywhere."

A hard edge entered Gallium's tone. "Except for my brother, I lost my entire family in the freeze. My mother...and my father died in the snow. King Carlomon was a decent king. Coldarius didn't deserve its fate. I imagine it was a terrible way to go. I've hated King Dubian ever since."

Gallium tied up his long hair with a piece of leather. "I was glad when your mother ended him. She made sure he suffered for a while before she put him out of his misery."

Prince Justin silently counted the packages of Callidut. "I've never agreed with taking a life unless there was no other option, but I understand how you feel. Had she killed him a bit sooner, maybe my father would still be alive.

"She was different before she ran away," said Gallium. "A bit angry, but not brutal. She was a good ChildForm. Losing you and your father changed her—twisted her heart. I know she's overjoyed that you're alive, but there's no turning back for her. She's an efficient killer. One would be a fool to cross her."

"Even me?" asked Prince Justin teasingly.

Gallium studied him for a long time before he spoke again. "I don't doubt she loves you, but if I were you, I wouldn't test the limits of her patience. Betrayal is the one thing she despises."

He stuck out his hand. Smiling, Gallium shook it.

"Thank you for letting me know, Gallium. I'll watch my back."

He looked over at Queen Aiki. "I'd better get her back to her bed chamber before she realizes what happened. The last thing I need is her getting in my way."

"Yeah, just make sure you don't end up in her bed. She's beautiful, but I hear quite a few MaleForms have entered and never walked out again."

"Trust me, I'm not that hard up for affection. She'll be sleeping alone."

A short time later, a sullen Queen Aiki accompanied General Revari to Earth. She had a throbbing headache but couldn't remember a thing. They had learned King Hitam had been living as Dr. Henrique Lattimer. They materialized in front of the hospital where he worked.

"Mount Caraman Hospital," read Queen Aiki. "This is it! You stay here. I'll go in and find him. I doubt he'll recognize me after all this time."

She was gone for a few moments before she returned, scowling fiercely. "Some idiot Human woman told me Hitam isn't here. He took a 'sick day.' What is that?"

"It means he stayed home from work," said General Revari.

"What is work?"

General Revari gave her a pointed look. In many ways, she had the innocence of a ChildForm. "Never mind. Please tell me you have the telepathic ability to find him. He's not a Platirian, so I can't."

She looked at her. "Telepathic ability?"

General Revari looked to the Heavens. "How am I going to kill him if you don't know how to connect with him? You haven't planned anything out! You just expected us to drop down on Earth and find him out of the blue?"

She smacked her teeth. "You've lived on Earth. You should know how to find him!"

"He's not a Platirian, you twit!"

They glared at each other for a moment. General Revari sighed. "I'll have to teach you how to connect with him. All family members share a psychic connection. We just need a quiet place to concentrate."

She pointed to a park across the street. "Over there. Follow me."

They sat face to face with their legs crossed. "Listen carefully. I want you to clear your mind and close your eyes. Concentrate on how King Hitam looked the last time you saw him."

"How long do I have to keep my eyes closed?"

"Until he materializes in front of you."

"What's that?"

General Revari struggled to hold on to what was left of her patience. "Until you can *see* him! If you concentrate hard enough, you will see him just as plainly as you see me."

Queen Aiki closed her eyes.

"Do you remember the last time you saw him?"

"Yes. I'll never forget that day."

General Revari nodded. Now they were getting somewhere. "All right, I want you to concentrate only on his face. Let your mind recall how he looked then. Allow your mind to expand."

"I...see him," said Queen Aiki slowly. "Something is happening. His face is changing. He looks...ancient."

"Yes," said General Revari excitedly. "Where is he?"

"He's sitting in a chair...in a...Human house. He's...reading papers." She frowned. "I feel his essence, but he's hiding in a Human shell."

"Where he's going, he won't need one. Concentrate harder, but don't let him feel the connection. When he starts glowing, grab my hand and we'll teleport to him."

"It's happening," said Queen Aiki, breathing rapidly. "He's glowing!"

General Revari grabbed her hand. "Let us go!"

Chapter 9

Queen Aiki opened her eyes and stared down at King Hitam. His appearance had changed drastically since she'd last seen him. His flesh was wrinkled and mottled. His hair, once thick and black, was thin, wispy, and gray. His dull eyes, surrounded by heavy bags, stared back at her.

"Who are you?" he demanded. "How did you get into my house?"

General Revari stared at him in shock. *This* ancient fossil was King Hitam? This was going to be too easy.

"I didn't expect you to remember who I was," said Queen Aiki. "After all, when you left Mother and I, you never looked back."

King Hitam's eyes grew large. "It...can't be!" he exclaimed. "Aiki? Get out! You don't belong here! I don't want my wife to find you here!"

General Revari couldn't believe her eyes. She'd expected to have a strong, vital opponent. Not a withered old buzzard. His murky eyes went from Queen Aiki to her.

"A Platirian!" he shouted.

As he stood, he changed from a badly aged old man to a tall, well-built MaleForm with bulging muscles. Pointing his sword at her, he said, "If you've come here to kill me, Platirian, I assure you, it won't be easy!"

"Now *this* is more like it!" said General Revari, bringing out her BrainStaff and sword. "Finally, I get to have some fun!"

Queen Aiki backed away. "Stay out of my way," General Revari warned her. You're not needed for this!"

Queen Aiki didn't have to be told twice. She hated fighting. She watched as they fought for what seemed like an eternity. She ducked as furniture and various items flew through the air. Finally, General Revari pinned him to the ground with the point of her BrainStaff. The house looked as if a cyclone had hit it.

An enraged King Hitam pinned her with a hateful gaze. "You brought our sworn enemy to kill me! I should've killed you before I left. You're a traitor to our race!"

"You brought this on yourself," said Queen Aiki. "This is what you're owed for hurting my mother!"

"She took her own life! What did it have to do with me?"

"Save your breath, King Hitam," said General Revari. "It's time to take your medicine."

"You Platirian whore! Had I killed King Dubian when I had the chance, you wouldn't be here right now!"

General Revari smiled. "I know." She leaned in closer to his face. "But you didn't." She beheaded him with a single swipe of her BrainStaff and threw back her head, allowing his energy to penetrate her. Her BrainStaff glowed as she absorbed all of the former king's power.

Queen Aiki clapped her hands together. "He is no more! You've sent him to Hell!"

She nodded and opened her eyes. They glowed a deep, vibrant red in the exuberance of the kill. "Queen Aiki," she said. "It's rude of you to send your father to Hell alone. It's time you acted like a proper lady."

Before Queen Aiki could blink, General Revari severed her head. She stretched out her arms as all the knowledge and strength of the former kings of Kikhani entered her. She was once again *Queen Revari*. Kikhani rumbled and churned as she took her rightful place as its new leader.

Kikhani shook with such a force, it knocked over everything around them. Gallium and Colonel Legend held on tightly to each other. When it finally stopped moving, Colonel Legend looked at Gallium.

"She did it!" she said, hugging him. "She's taken Kikhani!"

Gallium hugged her back. "Was there ever a doubt?" he asked. "We knew she'd get it done!"

Feeling the swell of her ample bosom against his chest, Gallium realized she was in his arms. Gently, he pushed her away. Now wasn't the time to get caught with his pants down. Literally.

"Are you still taking *Quinite*?" asked Colonel Legend.

"Legend!"

She gently pushed him. "Well, I'd like to know!"

He eyed her suspiciously. "Are you still taking it? That's what's more pertinent!"

She poked him in the chest. "Yes. I promised you I would, didn't I? I just think we should—you know—celebrate!"

Trying to ignore her dashing smile was difficult.

By The One, she's beautiful.

He stood, pulling her to her feet. "We'll celebrate when the time is right. Right now, we need to get this place cleaned up before Queen Revari returns."

"Queen Revari," said Colonel Legend. "I like the sound of that!"

Queen Revari appeared with a satisfied grin on her face. "Me too. And I like the sound of General Legend." The WomenForms laughed while Gallium rearranged his hair.

"Are you ready to be my general again?"

"I've been ready!" she said happily.

Gallium gave General Legend a *See how you almost got us into trouble?* look. When she stuck out her tongue at him, he quickly focused on getting the research chamber cleaned up.

"Good," said Queen Revari. "Let's get these Kikhanian clones acclimated to the new order of things. It's good to have a planet to run on again—a whole planet."

Gallium righted a bookshelf. "You've earned your place. You're just what Kikhani needs."

She scanned the perimeter. "Thank you, Gallium. Where's my son?"

"He's in the research chamber," Gallium told her. Whatever he was up to, he didn't want to get involved. It would be better to let her settle matters once she discovered what he was doing. Gallium guessed it wouldn't be long.

Rounds of applause sounded loudly as Captain Angela and Lieutenant Sheila were both promoted to colonel. Queen Revari proudly pinned medals on her two best warriors.

"Now that my army is growing, I'll need to split it down the middle to keep up with everyone. For your outstanding work on Earth and Kikhani, I'm overjoyed to present you with these medals of honor." Tears stood in the eyes of both WomenForms as she saluted them. "You've made me very proud."

Colonels Angela and Sheila vigorously shook hands with their leader and each other. They waved and blew kisses to their teammates and received thunderous cheers and well wishes.

"Kikhani is no more," announced Queen Revari. "Since I've conquered it and wiped out Queen Aiki and her clan, I'm naming it after me. This is now planet Revani!"

After thousands of years of separation, Gallium and General Legend were finally married under a bower of beautiful diamond and ruby roses. Dr. Barrios stood at his side as his best man, and Queen Revari stood as her maid of honor. Surrounded by love, the happy couple was celebrated by friends and family.

Finally, thought Queen Revari, *I feel as if I belong*.

She raised her glass in a toast to their new future together. "To the new Revaltians," she said.

"To us!" shouted everyone.

The Revaltians celebrated well into the early hours of dawn. For the first time in a very long time, she closed her eyes and slept peacefully.

Queen Vivant was finishing reports at her desk. A plate with a half-eaten turkey sandwich and potato salad sat near the edge. She reached for the sandwich and stopped.

A small bottle of CallePepper sat on the right of the plate. *This isn't possible*, she thought. After she'd shipped Simonius off, she'd ordered that all of the CallePepper be burned.

She was confident General Lyric had followed through. Sweating profusely, she got up from the desk. She had to be hallucinating again. When the dining staff had brought her lunch, there was no CallePepper. *Then where had it come from*? She reached for it before snatching her hand away.

If she touched it, she'd want to consume it. Was she dreaming? She rubbed her eyes hard and looked again. It was...gone! She drew out a shaky breath. She was pushing herself too hard. It was the only rational explanation she could think of for imagining the CallePepper had appeared.

Her appetite spent, she discarded the rest of her lunch into the trash bin. She needed rest. She'd nap and wake up refreshed and ready to resume her duties.

An eerie feeling claimed her as she opened the door to her bed chamber. Had someone been there? Quickly, she checked the enormous walk-in closets and bath chamber. She found nothing.

You're making yourself jumpy for nothing!

She removed her shoes, pulled back the covers, and got into bed, sinking into the fluffiness of the mattress. She closed her eyes and let out a deep breath. She'd been through a lot. She needed time to heal. She assured herself things would get better with time.

As she turned, she heard a sound. Sitting up in the bed, she looked around wildly, then listened. Nothing. She lay back down again and turned off the light, determined to calm her nerves.

"Mama..."

She sat up again and saw... No! It couldn't be!

"Mama..." the voice repeated.

From the edge of the bed, three hands reached out to her. Shakily, she turned on the light.

"Mama, help us," said Princess Tarah.

Hyperventilating, she gawked at her daughters in horror.

"Mama," said Princess Tyre. "We're dying!"

Purple liquid bubbled from two of the princesses' mouths as they fell to the floor. Princess Teenah pointed at her. "You killed us," she said.

Queen Vivant screamed.

Prince Justin smiled to himself. He'd infiltrated her mind while she was in her study. Teasing her with the CallePepper was already stimulating, but bringing her to hysterics was electrifying! General Lyric and a dozen soldiers came running to her aid. Concentrating, he locked the door so they couldn't enter.

"Queen Vivant!" said General Lyric. She tried turning the knob, but the door wouldn't open. "Are you hurt?"

He made Princess Teenah move toward Queen Vivant. She watched in horror as she crept toward her—the foul purple substance still oozing out of her mouth. The soulless look in her eyes made the queen's heart pound. Quickly, Teenah lashed out and grabbed her arm. Her touch was cold and clammy.

"You murdered us!" she whispered.

Queen Vivant screamed again.

General Lyric shouted, "We have to break down this door!"

The soldiers braced themselves to hurl their bodies against the door. Just as they sprang toward it, Prince Justin released it, and they went flying into her bed chamber. He thought he'd die from laughing when they ended up in a heap at the base of her bed.

General Lyric sprang quickly to her feet. "Queen Vivant! What's wrong?"

Her eyes darted around the bed chamber. "My daughters! They were here! They—they were dying of the Ashion all over again!"

General Lyric looked around the room. "Check the perimeter," she ordered.

The soldiers checked and returned in rapid time.

"There's nothing here, General," said Captain Kourtney.

"That's not true!" she cried. "They were lying right there where you're standing! Princess Teenah grabbed my arm!"

Sonee was on her way to the dining chamber for lunch when she heard the commotion. Something on the queen's nightstand caught her attention. Carefully, she picked up a small crystal bottle. She looked at Queen Vivant, then at General Lyric.

"What is it?" asked General Lyric.

"It's...CallePepper," Sonee reluctantly admitted.

Queen Vivant stared at the bottle in disbelief. "No! I haven't taken any Callidut—I swear! The bottle was in my study, but then it disappeared, and I came up here to lie down!"

Thirteen sets of eyes stared at her.

"I'm telling you the truth!" she shouted. "I'm not taking Callidut! It's been out of my system for a year!"

She looked around at the Platirian soldiers, her eyes pleading with them to believe her.

"I believe you," said General Lyric.

Sonee wasn't so sure. Queen Vivant's eyes were huge and she was covered in sweat. She looked exactly how she did when she'd been addicted to the CallePepper.

"Forgive me, Your Highness. How did it get in here?" asked Sonee.

"I—I don't know!" she said. "I'm telling you, I don't know. We burned it. Remember? There was none left!"

"Yes, we got rid of it," confirmed General Lyric. "And Gallium isn't here to make more, so where did it come from?"

"It could've been hidden in here somewhere," said Sonee, looking around. "Maybe one of the cleaning staff picked it up and put it on her nightstand."

"That's possible," said General Lyric. "Get it out of here. Let's do a clean sweep of the palace to make sure nothing is left." She turned to the other soldiers. "Remain posted outside Queen Vivant's bed chamber until I send your replacements."

The soldiers saluted her. "Yes, General!"

"Come with me, Sonee." General Lyric turned back to look at the queen. "It's going to be all right. You've come too far to turn back now. The worst is behind you."

But the worst was far from over. For many months, Prince Justin was relentless in his pursuit of making her lose her mind. He'd have a new set of clones appear in her bed chamber and in places where she'd least expect, then disappear just before the soldiers reached her.

Only she saw and felt what she thought were her daughters. Pretty soon, suspicions and accusations of her using Callidut began to surface despite vehement denials she hadn't returned to addiction.

Q ueen Vivant sat still as Sonee drew a blood sample. She had routinely tested the queen's blood, yet found no trace of the Callidut. The dining chamber had been subjected to numerous inspections of food and water supplies. Nothing was found.

Afraid of being poisoned again, she'd stopped eating properly and had lost a significant amount of weight. No matter how hard she tried, she couldn't eat or rest.

At times, she was found nodding in the gardens or standing on the balcony of her bed chamber, refusing to sleep. General Lyric and Sonee, appointed to Major after Queen Vivant assumed the reins of Platirius, were at a loss for how to handle the situation.

Although they tried to keep her torment from the rest of the Platirians, pretty soon gossip started buzzing around.

It became so out of hand that General Lyric reminded them of Queen Dellah's no-gossip decree. Anyone caught gossiping against a royal would be called in front of the justice council for creating a panic.

If they were found guilty of gossiping about a royal, they would be tossed into the Flames of Justice on the grounds of treason. The vicious rumors stopped. Immediately.

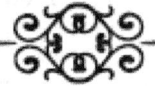

Prince Justin was getting impatient. Thoroughly irritated, he confided in Gallium. "She has a mind of steel!"

He kicked the nearest chair. "I've repeatedly set up the clones to die. She should've been rocking in a corner somewhere by now! And I position the Callidut right in front of her—just waiting for her to take it. But she hasn't. What more do I need to do?"

Gallium eyed him. "I think you need to leave it alone. You've got her in a position where she's afraid of her own shadow. You've accomplished what you set out to do."

He slammed a fist into his palm. "It's not enough, Gallium. I want to see her shattered into pieces. I'll never forgive her for what she did to my father."

His quest for vengeance against Queen Vivant was becoming an obsession. He couldn't see how it was changing him for the worse, but Gallium could. In an eerie way, he reminded him of King Dubian—hell-bent on causing harm to WomenForms.

It wouldn't be long before Queen Revari discovered what he was up to, but Gallium had no intention of telling her. She'd spared him and his brother from the Mass Deaths. Unfortunately, Dr. Barrios's luck had run out.

She'd executed him for providing Callidut to King Tylo. Gallium had no idea he'd been traveling to Pletz, and getting some of the WomenForms addicted. Callidut only altered the mental state of Platirians, but for Pletznians, it was lethal.

All of the WomenForms who consumed it had perished. King Tylo hadn't cared. He despised WomenForms. His reign was a stark contrast to the former king of Pletz, whose family had fostered love and respect among their subjects since the beginning of Pletz's time.

Dr. Barrios's job was to recruit more WomenForms into Queen Revari's army, but he'd been caught supplying them for Queen Vivant's army as well. It was also revealed that he had a long-time addiction to Callidut, thus rendering him useless to her. She'd wasted no time in beheading him.

Now, all of Gallium's family was dead. He mourned his brother briefly, then put it behind him. Swearing loyalty to a royal was a lifetime requirement.

Queen Revari abhorred betrayal. Gallium didn't believe she'd murder her own son, but he still walked a fine line. He didn't sympathize with Queen Vivant, but he was determined to survive. Finally granted the freedom to build a life with his long-time love, he had no time for petty games.

Prince Justin sighed. "Dr. Barrios's body was shipped off yesterday. Who will take his place to recruit more women?"

"I suppose she'll send General Legend," said Gallium.

He folded his arms. "But King Tylo hates women. It might be dangerous for her."

"WomenForms. If you're going to stay here for a while, start using our language properly. Using Human language places a glaring target on your back. As for my Legend, she's an excellent warrior. She can hold her own against MaleForms."

"Why not let me go to Pletz? Everyone has a job while I sit around and terrorize Queen Vivant. I want to help my mother get more recruits before I go back to Earth."

Gallium shook his head. "She won't let you get anywhere near him. If your identity is discovered, King Tylo will take your head without a second thought. Listen to reason. Stay on Revani where you're safe."

He smiled. "Why am I not surprised my mother renamed the planet after her? Okay, Gallium. I'll stay here like a good lad."

"Thank you. Queen Revari has enough issues to worry about."

His smile disappeared when Gallium left. "He makes it sound as if I'm an unwanted toddler," he said. He stole a craft and made his way to Pletz. "I'll prove my worth here. Then she'll let me stay."

King Tylo was much younger and better looking than he'd expected. And evil. A beautiful young WomanForm served their drinks. The king glanced at Prince Justin before grabbing her by the throat. Then he lifted her dress and roughly parted her legs with his knee.

Prince Justin watched in horror as King Tylo violated her, never taking his eyes off him. Her eyes bulged when he increased the pressure on her throat, displaying a viciousness that sickened him.

When he finished, he threw her to the ground and spat on her. Spent, he re-fastened his clothing and sat back in the chair, taking a long drink from his cup as the WomanForm hastily crawled away.

"Why should I help Queen Revari take Platirius?"

Prince Justin fought down his anxiety. The man was loathsome and crazy, but he'd get the job done. "If you joined forces, then you could share Platirius's wealth."

King Tylo sat forward in his chair and stared at him in amazement. Then he laughed. "Me? Share anything with a WomanForm? You can't be serious." His intense black eyes studied him with interest. "Where are you from?" he asked suddenly.

"From a neighboring planet," he lied. "Queen Revari captured my planet and forced me to work for her."

The king's dark eyes narrowed. "No," he said slowly. "I don't think that's true." His penetrating gaze seared into him, searching his mind.

Prince Justin felt a wave of dark energy flowing within him. Suddenly, a vision of King Tylo climbing out of a grave formed in his mind. He pushed and clawed at the dirt surrounding him.

His hands, raw and bleeding from punching his way out of the heavy death vessel, continued moving sediment out of the way until he made it to the top. He threw himself on the ground, struggling to get air into his lungs. The vision vanished just as quickly as it came. Prince Justin struggled to make sense of it, but couldn't.

Suddenly, King Tylo shifted in his chair. "You're a Platirian!" he said accusingly. "But how? Queen Vivant had three daughters, but I wasn't aware that Queen Revari bore a son!"

He jumped out of his chair. "You believe me stupid enough to hand Platirius over to you on a platter? If what you say about Queen Vivant is true, I have no problem killing her. But you? You'll die first! I won't let you sit on Platirius's throne!"

Prince Justin raised his hands in the air. "Calm down. I have no interest in becoming a king."

King Tylo grabbed his BrainStaff. "Then either you're a fool or you're lying! Either way, you won't leave Pletz alive."

He nodded to his soldiers. "Take him and kneel him down before me."

Prince Justin sneered. "Sorry, I didn't come here to die, my friend!"

King Tylo bellowed for the soldiers to stop him, but Prince Justin didn't stop running until he reached the craft. Using the power of Queen Revari's BrainStaff, he teleported himself back to Revani before King Tylo's soldiers could blink.

"No matter!" King Tylo said. "Once I kill Queen Vivant, I'll take Queen Revari's head along with her brat's! Soldiers! Prepare for Platirius!"

D ark clouds descended over Platirius as Queen Vivant struggled to remain focused. The visions of her daughters had stopped, but the damage had already been done. Word of her plight had spread to the justice council.

Chief Counselor Adoni sat with her in her meeting chamber. "Queen Vivant, the council wants to help, but we're at a loss. You have the power to heal everyone except yourself."

Queen Vivant's defeated demeanor saddened her. "You're the only Being permitted to go to the realm of The One for healing. We can appoint General Lyric to lead if you decide to step down and get treatment, but that's only a temporary solution."

The delicate cup clinked softly on the table as she set it down. "If word gets out that you're no longer leading Platirius, Queen Revari and rulers from other realms may attack us. General Lyric is strong, but she can't win against a combined attack. How will we survive without you here to protect us?"

Queen Vivant stared out a window. She could barely keep her eyes open. "I'm not going to The One's realm."

The Chief Counselor looked at her in astonishment. "Then what are you going to do? You cannot continue as you are. You'll crash and burn."

Queen Vivant wiped her eyes. "I don't know what to do," she said tearfully. "I know in spite of being tempted, I haven't used Callidut. I don't understand why the visions came. We've consistently tested our food and water supplies. There's no excuse for it other than dark magic."

Chief Counselor Adoni bit her lip. "Do you think Queen Revari is responsible?"

She turned to face her. "I didn't want to believe it at first. But no one hates me on the level she does. Who else would use my daughters against me in such a cruel way?"

"My Queen, we're under attack!" cried General Lyric.

Queen Vivant ran from the window. Hundreds of black crafts covered the sky, hovering menacingly over Platirius.

"Get to your stations!" she commanded. "Prepare to defend Platirius! Chief Counselor, find somewhere to hide! Planet Pletz is attacking us!"

The Chief Counselor quickly followed her instructions.

Queen Vivant snatched her BrainStaff off the wall. "The only way they'll take Platirius is if I die!" she promised.

Chapter 10

The battle between Pletz and Platirius lasted for months. King Tylo believed her to be weaker than Queen Revari, but she had proved him wrong. He had exhausted all the clones provided by Queen Aiki before she died.

He hadn't expected he'd need to use his Pletzarian soldiers, but he was out of options. Wounded, he lay behind a column and called in reinforcements, positioning them for an attack on his order.

"Queen Vivant!" he called. "I've only been toying with you. Your army has battled me for too long! They're tired and hurting. If I bring in my MaleForms, I'll take my time in killing you. Give up now and maybe I'll spare your life."

"It's you who should turn back, King Tylo! Pletz is smaller than us. You can't afford to lose your entire army against mine. There's no one to replenish your ranks!"

Suddenly, she saw three small figures approaching her.

No! Not now! Not when we're so close to victory!

"Mother," one said. "Will you kill us again?"

Another drew a sword. "Mother, come to me and die with honor. Let us go to Father."

"Noooo!" she screamed. "It isn't possible! You're not real! You're NOT real!"

King Tylo peered around the column at Queen Vivant. She was screaming into the air. He burst into laughter. "So it's true! You have spiraled into madness like your father! Finally, I can claim Platirius. Your legacy will end as nothing more than a crazy WomanForm, incapable of saving your Platirians!"

Sergeant Hiba breathed harshly as she struggled to tie a bandage tightly around General Lyric's thigh. Blood flowed heavily from a wound on her torso. "General, you have to stay still. If you keep moving, we may not be able to staunch the blood."

General Lyric's breath was ragged and uneven. "I can't, Sergeant Hiba. We've almost defeated him. We can't stop now."

They heard the sound of a blast from a BrainStaff and a scream. It was Queen Vivant.

With difficulty, General Lyric rose to her feet. "He's shot her with his BrainStaff!"

"General, please sit back down!" pleaded Major Sonee. "There's nothing we can do to help her if we all get killed!"

She looked up at the crafts. "He dispatched them from Pletz. He's just waiting to bring them in and kill us all."

King Tylo slowly approached her, dragging his right leg. "I'm going to enjoy taking Queen Revari's head, but ending your life will be all the sweeter," he said. "The prized daughter of King Dubian, now at my feet. Do you know how long I've waited for this day? To see you on your knees before me?"

Her eyes shifted around him, looking for her daughters, before fluttering back to him. He kneeled down in front of her, savoring every moment of her torment.

"Your sister isn't here to save you. What will you do now? Platirius is moments away from being rightfully ruled by a MaleForm."

He matched her frosty stare, then grinned. "You're being attacked by your own ChildForms. Well...in your head. No one can see them except you. Do you think it's right to allow a crazed WomanForm like you to rule Platirius?"

His wicked smile vanished. "You never should've been on the throne. It sickens me that Platirius's honor has been cheapened by WomenForms. Now you'll serve under me. You and all these WomenForms will do whatever I tell you to do."

Disgusted, he scrutinized the Vivacian soldiers. "If I want you to service me and my MaleForms, you'll do it with a smile. You'd be of better service as cleaning staff."

His black eyes, lined with long, heavy eyelashes, swept over them. Deep dimples on his cheeks and a small mole just above his top lip had lured more than a few unsuspecting WomenForms to his bed chamber.

It had been difficult for some of them to believe a MaleForm so handsome could be so evil—until it was too late. "I'll have you polishing my floors in the day and"—he raised his voice so that all could hear him—"using your lips to polish my treasure throughout the night! If your daughters were alive, I'd have fun with them too...right in front of you."

Her rage bubbled up and erupted as he laughed in her face. Her BrainStaff glowed blue when she hit him with a blast to the chest, knocking him high up into the air. He landed hard on the ground and cursed.

"I'LL HAVE YOU ON YOUR KNEES, QUEEN VIVANT! YOU WILL BOW TO ME AND BEG FOR MERCY!"

"You first, MaleForm!" said a sultry, low voice.

Everyone turned to see who had spoken. Queen Revari stood above Platirius with General Legend and thousands of Revaltians suspended on WarCrafts behind her. The Platirians gaped at the impressive sight.

She met Queen Vivant's eyes. Silently, the sisters assessed each other.

Better to be killed by her than a MaleForm, thought Queen Vivant.

Queen Revari raised her BrainStaff in the air. "Someone should've told you, King Tylo, there's only one who'll have Queen Vivant's head. Me." Pointing her BrainStaff at him, she bellowed, "REVALTIANS! KILL THAT MALEFORM! FOR PLATIRIUS!"

Queen Vivant let out a long breath. Energized, she stood. "FOR PLATIRIUS!"

General Lyric and Sergeant Hiba screamed and charged forth as a collective roar from the Revaltian and Vivacian soldiers sounded.

King Tylo stared at them in disbelief. *Didn't the hybrid say she would help me defeat Queen Vivant?*

He didn't have time to make sense of it as WomenForm soldiers on both sides attacked him. Queen Vivant picked up her BrainStaff and swung at him. General Lyric and General Legend valiantly fought side by side. The writing was on the wall for him as the WomenForms sent him an unequivocal message: Platirius would *not* have a MaleForm ruler that day or any day!

He fought back, wounding and killing as many as he could, but he was overpowered by the WomenForms. His maniacal laugh rang out with each hard blow he took. He was outnumbered, but his deeply ingrained insanity made him delusional enough to believe he could still win.

The soldiers could feel the momentum of what was coming. The morale of the Platirians soared at the prospect of defeating King Tylo and conquering Pletz.

He fell at Queen Vivant's feet, laughing out of sheer hatred for the WomenForms. "You soulless whores! Your worthless father stole my birthright. I am the rightful leader of Platirius! I'm not leaving here until I spit on your burned carcasses!"

"Did you hear what he said?" asked General Legend. General Lyric nodded. Long before Queen Dellah married King Dubian, Platirians were buried in the ground inside their DeathCrafts.

Queen Revari and Queen Vivant stared at him. "Queen Vivant!" said Queen Revari. "He's Prince Dimaro!"

Eerily familiar black eyes penetrated her. Wiping his bloody mouth on his black sleeve, he said, "That's right, you wretched little whore. Soon to be King Dimaro! I'm going to enjoy cutting you and your sister's heads off, and I hope your father is watching from hell!"

His evil laugh rang over the courtyard. "Did you think I came here alone? That's the problem with WomenForms—your intellect is nonexistent. This is why MaleForms are better suited to lead! Take a look above you and tell me if you've defeated me!"

All eyes looked to the army of Pletzarians suspended above them. He laughed again. "Oh, you had a good run! I'll give you that!" He wiped away the blood gushing from a wound on his head. "You look precious in your little uniforms playing war. But now, it's time to end this. Do you really think my army will stand and watch me fall?"

"Yes, we will," said General Absalom.

Startled, King Tylo swung around to look up at him. "What did you say, General?"

"You heard me the first time. Pletzarians, stand down."

At their general's command, every Pletzarian soldier lowered their weapons.

Spittle flew from King Tylo's lips. "You fool! You'd betray me for a bunch of WomenForms?"

General Absalom met his furious gaze. "It's not WomenForms we have a problem with. It's you. Pletz was a peaceful planet until you repaid my father's kindness for taking you in by murdering him in his bed. We have always treated our WomenForms with love and respect. But you forced your wickedness on us."

The general pointed his sword at him. "You conspired with that disgraceful Dr. Barrios to get our WomenForms addicted to Callidut—sending them into madness before they perished. The ones you didn't kill were sold to replenish Queen Revari and Queen Vivant's armies after Platirius became whole again."

He pointed at a group of Vivacians standing off to the side. "Some of my soldiers' ChildForms are standing before you. Do you think they'd slay their own daughters?"

"If I were you, I'd be careful, General Absalom. I am Pletz's king now. You're committing treason! Pletzarians, seize him!"

To his amazement, none of the Pletzarian soldiers moved. General Absalom shook his head. "They won't listen to you. We've grown weary of your darkness. You know nothing of what it means to love and cherish WomenForms!"

Years of suppressed anguish clouded the general's bearded face. "Without them, our population has dwindled to nothing! All that's left are the MaleForms standing before you. You destroyed our families. Our home. It will be my honor to see your head taken."

King Tylo glared at the WomenForms, then at General Absalom. "You idiot! Then Pletz will be absorbed into Platirius! Is that what you want?"

General Absalom nodded firmly. "That's exactly what I want. Nothing is left of Pletz except the essence of my ancestors. Deep memories of millions of years of love and respect between the SexForms will proliferate the grounds of Platirius, cleansing the corruption set by your ancestors."

King Tylo looked at all of the Pletzarian soldiers, unable to believe what he was hearing.

"The merge will bring healing to Platirius—giving its race and ours a fresh start," said General Absalom. "Yes, I am in favor of helping King Dubian's daughters finish what he started. We've come to watch you die today."

Enraged, King Tylo shouted, "After all I've done for you!"

"What have you done for our benefit? Look at the pain in the faces of my soldiers. You see these WomenForms as objects to exploit and murder. My soldiers see the daughters they lost as babes that grew up without them. You had no right to tear their families apart. Today, they will finally receive justice."

General Absalom addressed Queen Vivant. "I'd be honored to serve under you. Yes, we are MaleForms, but we are peaceful. We are nothing like your ancestors. Our honor comes from provision and protection—not oppression. We won't defend him."

"Platirius is mine. It's always been mine. King Dubian tried to bury me deep in the ground, but I refused to allow it. I didn't climb my way out of that hole to allow his brats to kill me again! I will have my vengeance against my brother! DO YOU HEAR ME?!"

Queen Revari had heard enough. "Take hold of him, Revaltians. Get him on his knees."

Standing beside Queen Vivant, she said, "It began with Platirius and will end with it."

She stepped back as Queen Vivant stepped forward.

Raising her BrainStaff high in the air, Queen Vivant said, "You should've stayed in that hole. Now your DeathCraft will read that you were killed by a WomanForm. To someone like you, the shame of that is worse than death itself!"

She sliced off his head in one clean blow. All the power of Platirius and Pletz's legacy rose and soared into Queen Vivant and Platirius. The long history of dysfunction and chaos had come full circle.

The absorption brought a new mindset to the WomenForms of Platirius. No longer did they despise and fear MaleForms. The stolen daughters of Pletz rushed to their fathers, embracing them as they wept for joy. Finally, the long years of oppression had ended.

Queen Vivant turned to Queen Revari. "Platirius and Revani are of equal power now. Will you merge peacefully with us and come home?"

She shook her head. "I have a home now. I've never been welcome on Platirius."

Queen Vivant's eyes glistened with tears. "Then...you're here to fight me for the throne?"

"No, Vivant. I'm no longer interested in leading Platirius. That honor belongs to you now."

"No!" said Prince Justin. *What is she doing?* "Mama! This is the perfect time! She doesn't trust her own mind. She's not fit to run Platirius! Kill her!"

"Had you not interfered, maybe I would have taken it all. If it weren't for you and King Tylo working together to bring her down, she wouldn't be in the state she's in. You had to cheat to get her off her game."

Her silver eyes took in the badly damaged and burned buildings. "If I take Platirius now, my efforts will only be putting the finishing touches on the plans MaleForms set to be victorious over a WomanForm. That goes against every code I believe in."

She turned to Queen Vivant. "It seems my son is more like me than I realized." She stretched out her arm, wielding the power of her BrainStaff.

Queen Vivant sucked in her breath and sank to her knees. "No, no, no," she whispered. "It's happening again!"

Everyone watched in astonishment as Princess Teenah, Princess Tyre, and Princess Tarah joined Queen Revari.

"It's the princesses!" cried Major Sonee. "She really was seeing them!"

"No," said Queen Revari. "Prince Justin devised a cruel plan to drive her mad. He used Queen Aiki's clones to deceive her into believing she was being punished by her dead daughters."

She looked down at Queen Vivant, still kneeling on the ground. "I've waited years to see you like this—groveling before me, driven out of your mind. Now that day has come, but it doesn't bring me the joy I thought it would."

She reached down and helped her to her feet. "You are the Queen of Platirius," she said coolly. "Collect your decency enough to face me."

Bewildered, Queen Vivant looked at Queen Revari, then looked at the young WomenForms standing at her side and sobbed uncontrollably. "Make them go away, please!" she begged. "I can't take it!"

"Stop your blubbering! These aren't clones! They are your real daughters. They never died. I only made it look like they did. Do you remember what I told you when you broke into my palace on Rubarius?"

Terrified, Queen Vivant shook her head. She was so confused, she no longer remembered breaking into Queen Revari's palace to kill her.

"I said it would be more fun to put them in my army and watch them suffer while I dethroned you. I did exactly what I said I would. I defeated you with the Callidut and the clones I received from Queen Aiki to make you think they were dead."

She forced Queen Vivant to meet her gaze. "They watched while you went in and out of sanity, and there was nothing they could do to help you. They had to take orders from me and go wherever I told them to go. They helped me collect the souls required to take over Earth."

The princesses moved closer to Queen Vivant, who would've stepped back had Queen Revari not held her in place.

"And they helped me rebuild Kikhani, transforming it into Revani. They've been fighting by my side all this time. I didn't give them a choice. If any of them made a wrong move, your life would be forfeit. They loved you too much to risk losing you."

Queen Vivant couldn't believe her senses. It had to be another trick. She saw her daughters die right before her eyes!

"You took away my family. My husband and my baby," said Queen Revari. "I wanted you to suffer—to know how it felt to lose a ChildForm. But I have my son again. Even though I'm displeased with his actions, I now know how it feels to be a MotherForm."

Prince Justin glared at Queen Vivant, blatantly unremorseful for what he'd done to her.

"He has his faults and doesn't realize the severity of the threat he brought upon Platirius today, but he's alive. I get to see him, touch him, and talk to him."

Queen Revari looked at her son. "Now that I have him again, I no longer wish to punish you by keeping your daughters away from you. Look at them. They're healthy and strong. I have not harmed them."

Using both hands, she turned Queen Vivant's head toward her daughters. "I've taught them how to fight and defend Platirius, instead of being pampered, spoiled brats. And I've earned their respect as a military leader."

It was true. Pride shone in the princesses' eyes as they stared at their aunt and former leader standing with their mother—the two WomenForms they loved most.

"Now they are ready to return to you and defend Platirius's honor. I have my own life to live and my own planet to run. Don't shun them, Vivant. You need them now."

But Queen Vivant refused to believe they were real. The shadows cast on her sanity by Prince Justin were still too potent.

General Lyric looked at him. "How could you have done this to her?"

His handsome face clouded with rage. "It's what she deserved for helping to kill my father. She had it coming."

"It was me who rejected you, not her. If you were angry and wanted revenge, you should've taken it out on me!"

He looked at her as if the sun set and rose just for her. "Why would I do that? I hate her, but, Lyric, I—I could never hurt you. If only you'd allow yourself to see how I feel about you."

He raised his hands in the air. "I get it. You love Platirius. But isn't there room in your heart for something else? Haven't you ever wanted more than taking orders from her?"

"No, I haven't. I've never had any feelings for a MaleForm until..."

She stopped herself before she went too far. He waited.

"Until what, Lyric? Go ahead and finish. Tell me I'm the only one who can't sleep at night. Do you think you can say it with a straight face?"

They stood face to face—there was so much she wanted to say but couldn't. Platirius was her home and her pride. Nothing in the universe could make her abandon it. And...after what he did, she could never trust him.

"This little scene is touching, but General Lyric? If you don't back away from my son, Prince Dimaro won't be flying into the sun alone today."

"Mama, stay out of this!"

"I'm staying out of nothing! This is Platirius, not Earth. And that WomanForm," she said, pointing at General Lyric, "will die before I allow you to be with her."

"Wow...what an ego. Do you hear yourself? Who do you sound like, Mama? How can you say that after what King Dubian did to you and my father?"

"This is an entirely different situation. General Lyric is my enemy. Your father was innocent—she isn't. There's no way I'm letting her get close to you. And after the stunt you pulled, I doubt she wants anything to do with you now."

He looked to General Lyric. "Is that true? Is being your crazy queen's puppet still the only thing that makes you happy?"

Deeply offended, she looked him up and down. "I'm no puppet. I am the General of Platirius. I don't expect that to mean anything to you, but protecting my planet means everything to me."

He grabbed her shoulders. "This isn't your planet, Lyric. King Dubian destroyed your real home, Coldarius. He killed *your* father. She helped him murder *my* father. How could you be proud to work for someone as evil as she?"

She shrugged off his strong grasp. "She isn't King Dubian. And *if* it's true, I don't blame her for what he did. You want to talk about evil? You altered her mind and used clones to inflict the worst pain she's ever experienced. How could you ask such a question?"

Pointing a finger in his chest, she said, "What you did was beyond cruel. If you expect me to turn a blind eye to it, I can't. This ends now."

She walked over to Queen Vivant and stood by her side.

"I guess I have my answer, huh? I should've known you'd never be with me."

Queen Revari stood in front of him. "That's irrelevant compared to what you've done. Due to your actions, a MaleForm, a descendant of King Anemi, almost took the throne of Platirius. You can't begin to comprehend the ramifications of your actions!"

He unconsciously took a step backward—angered by the force behind her words.

"Had your plans succeeded, it would have set Platirius back millions of years!" said Queen Revari. "All the work Queen Vivant and I have done would've been for nothing. I told you, this is no place for you. You do not understand our ways. You could've ruined everything!"

His eyes filled with angry tears. "Well, if I'm such a disappointment to you, Mama, why don't you send me back to Earth so you won't have to look at me. Everything I've done was to help you!"

She shook her head. "You weren't trying to help me. You wanted to get back at her. It wasn't your place to deal with her. It was mine!"

He pointed at the princesses. "What about you? You had her believe her daughters were dead! How are you any better than I?"

She raised an eyebrow. "I know the rules of the game, ChildForm. I planned to become the sole ruler of Platirius. I succeeded until The One intervened. But General Lyric doesn't want you now. Where is the prize *you* coveted, son?"

"Don't call me that. Not when you're taking her side over mine. I never want to see you again. Send me home. To my *real* mother!"

He said it to hurt her, and it did. Mercilessly.

"Fine," she said softly. "I release you from this world."

Instantly, he disappeared. He woke up in his condo alone. Seizing a heavy paperweight, he whirled it into a mirror. The glass shattered as he sank to his knees. He'd lost the women he loved—his mother and General Lyric. He wished he'd never seen Platirius.

Queen Vivant's eyes darted around feverishly. She had to get away from the monsters! Fast!

"Mother," said Princess Tyre. "It truly is us! Please don't be afraid."

She reached out to touch her mother, but she instinctively shrank away from her.

"She doesn't believe we're real," said Princess Teenah mournfully.

"I want to return to the darkness," whispered Queen Vivant. "I want to rest now."

General Lyric started to go to her but was stopped by Queen Revari's raised hand.

"Allow them to handle this," she told her.

Princess Tyre said, "Mother, if you go into the dark, I won't be able to follow you. I'm afraid of the dark, remember? Come, let us sing the song you sang to me when I was afraid. Do you remember the words?"

She shook her head. Princess Tyre began to sing. It was a song her mother made up for her one night when she couldn't sleep. Only she and Princess Tyre knew the words.

Memories of staying late into the night by her daughter's bedside until she slept came flooding back. Tentatively, she joined Princess Tyre in singing a few bars until mother and daughter sang the entire song together. Tears of joy glistened in the eyes of all around them, except for Queen Revari and her clan.

"You made her think her daughters were dead. Have you no shame?" asked General Lyric.

General Revari closed the distance between them. "The day I answer to you is the day I stop being royalty. That's not going to happen anytime soon."

"It will if you're arrested for crimes committed against Platirius!"

Incandescent, mysterious flames ignited in her eyes. "Who's going to arrest me, General?"

"Let it go, General Lyric," said General Legend. "The feud is between them—it doesn't concern you. If Queen Vivant wants to come for us, we'll be ready. But it will be her decision—not yours."

The princesses embraced their mother as she wept, wrapping them tightly in her arms.

"We're even, Queen Revari," she sobbed. "Please let us finally put an end to this now."

The crimson fire in Queen Revari's eyes flickered softly. "Oh no...we'll never be even. I'm letting you have today. I wouldn't read any more into it."

"Sister, please? I love you. Mother wants you to come home," she pleaded. She moved forward to embrace her.

Queen Revari stepped out of her reach. "My son really succeeded in driving you crazy, didn't he? Mother has nothing to do with this. She's dead—just like my husband. You remember him, don't you?"

Queen Vivant winced.

"Be thankful I'm being merciful today, Vivant. I won't always be. Revaltians! Let us return home!"

In the arms of her daughters, Queen Vivant watched as the crafts flew across the galaxy, disappearing among the stars.

"Mother, we never had the chance to have our LifeCelebration," said Princess Tarah. "Those creepy clones were programmed to act like us. We had to sit and watch the whole thing!"

Queen Revari believed she hadn't hurt them due to keeping their bodies intact. But the psychological damage she'd inflicted on them was far worse than physical wounds. Queen Vivant knew she'd need to work hard to use her healing powers for them to be whole again.

Gazing at the new additions to Platirius, she said, "Then today is a perfect day to have one. A Celebration of Life for all of us. After all we've been through, we certainly deserve one, yes?"

Inspired by the queen's words, everyone regarded each other with renewed hope.

"But first, we must dispose of Prince Dimaro. General Absalom, please get him into a DeathCraft and let's get him off Platirius. Then we'll clean up this mess and have a feast. How does that sound?"

Her declaration was met with cheers and rounds of hugs. It was a new beginning for Platirius—one filled with faith and the promise of a better, brighter future.

She didn't know when she'd see Queen Revari again—whether they'd still be foes or would finally come together as sisters.

At the moment, her focus was on her daughters and all the citizens of Platirius. For now, that was enough.

Coldarius: The Origin of Gallium Book I

On Platirius, Princess Dellah was having a luncheon of a different kind—with the heads of Platirius's chambers. Wanting to ensure she got off on the right foot with the Platirians, she'd summoned them together for an important meeting. As their future queen, it was imperative for everyone to be clear on her expectations.

She sat in King Dubian's high chair, allowing her feet to dangle underneath the enormous desk. "Thank you all for coming today. I know how busy you are, so I'll get right to the point. There is far too much in-fighting and gossiping going on. Not only within the work chambers, but inside the palace as well. I've heard that not only did King Anemi and Queen Zherta make no effort to stop it, they encouraged it. That will no longer be the case."

She looked around at the crowd to make sure she had their attention. "On Coldarius, we live and work as one unit. As a team. We do not have time nor have my father and I ever made time for pettiness. We all know I wasn't born on Platirius. However, I will become a Platirian very soon."

Holding their stares with ease, she said, "Let me assure you, I intend for the peaceful harmony Coldarians enjoy to be extended to Platirius as well. For the first time in history, I will select a group of my trusted staff to accompany me to live here. I expect nothing less than harmonious relationships fostered between Coldarians and Platirians."

Some of the Platirians began whispering among themselves. They'd expected her to be a meek, self-depreciating WomanForm who would do King Dubian's bidding without question. They had just discovered they were wrong.

She waited for the whispering and shifting around to stop. "As of today, I'm issuing a no-gossiping decree. No longer will Beings be forced to suffer under malicious gossip and shattered reputations. If one has grounds for slander, the tormentor will be called to stand in before the justice council. If one is found guilty of slander, the victim will be awarded everything you own. And I mean everything."

Shocked, angry glares darted at her as furious whispers spread among the spectators. She ignored them. "If you cannot prove what you say or have nothing nice to say about your neighbors, then it's best to say nothing at all."

Ana Weiss chuckled maliciously. "I have nothing nice to say about any of you," she whispered. A few evil chuckles rang out among her small group of supporters.

"What's that you said, Ana Weiss?" asked Princess Dellah. "If you have something relevant to add, then please stand and say it to my face."

Ana gasped. She didn't think the Princess had heard her. Haughtily, she stood. "I meant no disrespect, Princess Dellah."

Princess Dellah's silver eyes resembled chips of ice. "Then what did you mean, Ana? Obviously, it was important enough to rudely interrupt my meeting. I'd like to hear you make your statement out loud."

Ana bristled, clearly offended by the Princess's imperious tone. "It's not that serious, Your Highness," she said frostily.

The spectators looked from Ana to Princess Dellah. Ana was related to General Sodom. That made Beings fear her. She knew it and willfully used it to her advantage. Everyone waited to see if her boldness would place the first crack in the Princess's power. They didn't have to wait long.

"The only thing I see frivolous here is you," said Princess Dellah coldly.

A few gasps let out in the crowd.

"Silence," she hissed. "I don't want to hear another sound." Her eyes found Ana again. The fierceness in them made Ana unconsciously take a step back.

"Now, you may think your family's position gives you power, but let me assure you, I have no problem shipping you and your entire lot off Platirius. And if you don't think I'll do it, I invite you to test the limits of *my* power."

Ana's face clouded in fury. She pointed at her. "You're not the Queen of Platirius yet! You're a Coldarian. You have no business telling us what to do or when to do it! If you want to control something, stay in your place until you marry King Dubian. Until then, the little power you *think* you have only exists in your pretty little head."

Princess Dellah rose from the impressive desk. "Oh? You think so? Well, if that's what's going on in your confused, *decrepit* head, allow me to get you and everyone here straight. Right now. Guards."

Immediately, three Platirian soldiers appeared. "Yes, Princess Dellah? How may we be of service?"

She pointed to Ana. "Drag her out of this chamber and get her into a craft. Then, I want you to root out everyone related to her—and I do mean everyone—except General Sodom—and toss them into the craft with her."

Eyes blazing, she turned to Ana. "We're about to find out whether I *think* I have power or whether I *know* I do. I want everyone cleared out of here and standing at the center of the palace in five minutes." She scanned the crowd. "Don't make me come looking for you."

The crowd quickly cleared out of the meeting chamber, tripping over each other to get to the door. The soldiers grabbed Ana and forcibly ushered her and her family into a craft.

A few of the Coldarian soldiers who had accompanied the Princess stood by awaiting her orders. "Where shall we program the craft to go, Princess Dellah?" asked General Iham.

She held up a hand and turned to a visibly shaken General Sodom. "Do you have anything to say, General Sodom?"

He coughed and shook his head furiously. "No, Princess Dellah! Before King Dubian left for Coldarius, he said you're now in charge of the military. I answer only to you!"

She nodded. "That's a good dog, Sodom."

She turned back to face Ana. Terrified, she stared out a window at her. Princess Dellah's deadly gaze never wavered from the older WomanForm. She said, "General Sodom, send that craft into the sun."

He saluted her. "Yes, Your Highness!"

Ana screamed when the craft powered up for launch. The startled Platirians watched in horror as it lifted into the air and flew rapidly toward the sun. The screams of terror subsided when it sank into the sun and burst into flames. She smiled and turned back to the crowd.

"My gossip decree will be enforced starting today. Anything said against a member of a royal family, or any show of force against one, shall be considered treason and will be met with immediate death. In either case, no trial will be heard before the justice council. You and your entire families will be tossed into the Flames of Justice or—" she looked at the sun again "—introduced to my new favorite way of taking out the trash—burned in the heart of the sun."

Waves of shock reverberated between the Platirians as they met her chilly gaze. "I have an abundance of respect for you Platirians. I want you to respect me too." Her brilliant platinum eyes sliced through the crowd. "But I wouldn't test the limits of my patience. The consequences...may prove to be fatal. Does anyone else have something to add?"

No one dared to breathe as she waited. She nodded. "Very well, you may return to your duties. I'm looking forward to a new Platirius—one that is prosperous and joyous for all of us. Those who do not understand my vision needn't worry about staying around to see it. Have I been heard?"

The Platirians didn't hesitate. "Yes, Princess Dellah!"

She flashed a dazzling smile at them. "Thank you for allowing me to join Platirius. I am looking forward to building a new reign with King Dubian."

D.L.'s Note

D ear Reader,

You've finally taken a third journey to Platirius! What did you think of the ending? Were you surprised to see another male member of the Amorous family causing havoc?

I just couldn't let the series go another round without giving you a glimpse of how Platirius would be if a queen wasn't at the top. And how about Queen Aiki? Wasn't she a hoot?

I thoroughly enjoyed developing the Queen of Kikhani. She was loads of fun! Platirius III took a lot out of me. I was under a lot of pressure to close up Platirius I and II with a neat bow. Is this the end of the Platirius series?

At this time, I'm not saying yea or nay. I like leaving open doors to explore not only for you, the reader, but for myself as well. Get ready for my brand new series: Coldarius.

The prequel to Platirius is locked and loaded with action and has the most boldest, larger than life characters I've ever written. If you want to see where Queen Revari gets her fearlessness and why Queen Vivant is the calmer, more collected sister, stay tuned for the fascinating world of Coldarius!

Be easy!

xoxo D.L.

Join my VIP List

Get the latest info on new releases, giveaways, and free
promotional goodies at www.dlhannah.com!

Author Bio

D.L. Hannah was born in Youngstown, Ohio. She is a writer, entrepreneur, and host of the Amerisogyny podcast. She is a Psi Chi and Alpha Kappa Delta member and earned a Bachelor of Arts degree in Clinical Community Psychology from Walsh University. For over twenty years, she has been a strong advocate for children diagnosed with Autism. She now lives in North Carolina with her family.

Also by D.L. Hannah

Platirius: Infiltration Book I
Platirius: The Rise of Reve Book II
Platirius: Kikhani vs Platirius Book III
Coldarius: The Origin of Gallium Book I
Coldarius: The Betrayal Book II
JanIus: Pawns Book I
JanIus: Enter the King Book II
JanIus: Platirius vs JanIus Book III
Maieman: Paradox Book I
Maieman: Revelations Book II